BY THE LIGHT OF THE MOON

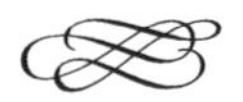

CINDY NICHOLS

CHAPTER 1

Orange and blue flames shot high in the night sky as Colin stood in the fire station, waiting for the other volunteer firefighters to arrive. The call had gone out all over the South Campos, a loose-knit community covering a long span of beach on the northern Sea of Cortez, in Baja California. The large American population relied on the marine radio to keep in touch, and the emergency had been broadcast to all. Now, the volunteer firefighters were rushing in. He hoped that someone was already at least dousing the flames with hoses or buckets.

"Bomberos, bomberos, fire at Campo Ventana." His hands clenched tightly as the men he had helped train quickly and silently donned their turn-outs. The truck was ready to go, filled with water, as there would likely be little water available at the fire scene. His stomach already in knots and adrenaline flooding his veins, he was eager to be off to the scene, wondering how much damage had already been done.

The men, his friends and fellow firefighters, were ready in a flash and seated on the truck. The captain gave Colin a nod, and with that, he started the engine, flipping the switch for the siren and lights as soon as he'd pulled out of the garage that served as a fire station in this remote, seaside community.

His stomach churned as he watched the flames grow, speeding toward the structure as fast as was possible on the dirt road he'd turned down, expecting a mile at least of a bad trek into the campo. The fire was closer to the water, the Sea of Cortez, and the truck bounced on the ruts and stones. Colin's fist pounded on the steering wheel as he was forced to slow down.

"This camp doesn't have a well," his friend James grumbled, a fact that had already caused Colin's chest to tighten with worry.

"You're right, but we have a full truck and can call for the second. Hopefully, they've already started emptying their water tanks on it."

Firefighting in the Baja California community of

the South Campos was a challenge as most areas had to have water delivered, and it was a valuable commodity. Here, along the beaches of the Sea of Cortez, a few of the camps had wells, but not this one. Homeowners had large water tanks on the roofs of their houses and water was delivered and used sparingly.

On the occasions that a fire did break out, everybody in the campo pitched in to help. Bucket brigades and hoses backed up the firefighters, hoping that the fire would be contained to one small area and the whole campo wouldn't go up in flames. As Colin neared the fire, he hoped this would be one of the lucky times that it wouldn't.

The full moon shone brightly on the road, and they were able to find their direction with its help. Colin was grateful for that. There were no streets to speak of, the dirt roads leading to the homes in the area difficult to navigate. Colin let out a sigh of relief as he saw that this particular garage that was on fire was right by the road, and there was no risk of getting the fire engine stuck in the sand that some roads were plagued with. The flames shot high into the sky.

"James, take Colin and Javier with you with the

fire hose and start. I'll go help the owner on the other side with their hoses."

"Got it," James said as he motioned for the men to follow him. They'd already gotten the fire hose out and were ready to roll.

"Over here," a woman shouted as Colin headed to the opposite side of the building. A man and a woman stood with a hose that sprayed not much more than a trickle on the flames. "We're so glad you're here. We're doing what we can," she said, her hand leaving a trail of soot as she brushed her hair out of her eyes.

The roof of the brick garage was engulfed in flames and Colin ushered the owners back toward the house as the spray of the fire engine hose did its job. "Is there anyone in danger? Anyone in the garage?" he asked as the man sat down with a thud and stared at the garage.

"No, no one in there. Humans and animals accounted for."

Colin said a silent thanks that this one looked simple and no one was in harm's way. As the flames subsided, he walked to the other side of the building. Branches rustled as he passed a tree back a bit from the building, out of sight from the house. "Who's there?" he yelled, hoping it was his imagination.

His eyes widened as the shape came slowly into view by the light of the dying flames. His eyes narrowed as he tried to make sense of what he saw. Out of the shadows came a woman, her hair black and long, her eyes dark and beautiful. He wondered at the riding boots and jeans for a moment until he saw what followed her. The horse she led behind her whinnied as he stopped directly behind her, his head raised at the flames.

"You shouldn't be here," he said, starting toward her to lead her away. "Horses don't like fires, and you could be hurt."

She held her hand up, stopping him in his tracks. "My horses know when they are safe," she said. "And she is safe now. We wanted to see if we could help."

He stood still a moment, not quite sure what to say. The horse was beautiful, with a long black mane and shiny coat. He had raised horses as a child in Ireland but had never seen one that remained calm around fire. "I don't see how you could, but thank you. Horses and fires don't mix."

Her lips curved into a smile, one eyebrow raising as she glanced at the mare beside her. "You don't know my horses." She smiled back at him as she settled her foot in the stirrup and swung her leg over the beautiful mare. Nodding her head in his direction, they turned and were swallowed by the darkness.

"Who was that?" James asked as Colin came around to the truck. "Was that a horse?"

"Aye, it was. I don't know who she was or where she came from. She wanted to see if she could help."

"With a horse? At a fire?" He slapped his forehead with his hand. "What was she thinking? Horses and fire don't mix."

"That's what I told her, but she didn't seem to agree." Colin looked into the distance to see where she had gone, but the flames had gone and the darkness taken over.

CHAPTER 2

The fire was completely knocked down with not even a wisp of smoke remaining. "Nicely done, lads," Colin said, slapping his newest crew member on the back and offering his hand.

"That one wasn't too bad," Robert said as he shook Colin's hand. "Glad nobody was hurt." The young man's freckled face shone with sweat as he wiped his brow with a red neckerchief. "I've seen much worse where I come from."

Colin turned back toward the building. "It sure could have been worse."

"Yeah, much worse," Robert said as he walked toward the engine.

"Good on you, mates," Colin called out to the rest

of the crew as he turned toward the owner approaching the rubble.

The owner of the garage walked around the side of the building, stepping gingerly over the charred remains of beach chairs, kayaks and fishing rods. "Thank you, boys. You were here in a hurry. So glad it didn't get over to the house."

"That's what we try for, sir. Keep it as small and contained as possible." Colin took his offered hand and gave it a strong shake.

"The wife and I had a bad feeling when we heard the firecrackers going off on the beach. What with the breeze and all, it's not a good idea. They could land on anyone's roof and it's all over."

"You heard fireworks tonight?" Colin hadn't noticed any, but there were many miles of beach and lots of people loved fireworks, oblivious to the danger to the homes they lived in.

"Yes, we've heard them for several nights. Some out-of-towners on vacation. They've been riding up and down the beach and having fireworks every night. We asked them to move further on, but they wouldn't.

"I can come back tomorrow and take a look. Maybe I can see what started it if you're really not sure."

"I don't know for sure if it was the kids and their fireworks. Easy to blame them, though. I don't know what else it could have been. I'd appreciate it if you'd check."

"I'm not exactly a professional, but I'd be happy to take a look."

The man and his wife glanced quickly at each other. "We've heard that you might know a thing of two about fires. We'd appreciate the help."

Colin hung his head in mock shame as he heard James roar with laughter.

"Yes, his experience with the IRA should come in handy."

"Thanks, James. That's all I need."

The man and his wife grabbed for each other's hands. "Well, we've heard things."

"Have you, now," Colin replied with his thickest Irish accent. "I hope I can live up to your expectations." He couldn't help but smile as he turned away and saw the glee on James' face.

"Careful, friend. Next thing you know, they'll be calling you because there's a spy in the house. 007, to the rescue."

Laughter filled the cab of the fire engine as the men returned to the station. It was always a relief to successfully put out a fire and they shared a collective sense of relief that no one had been hurt. A cheer rang out as Colin said, "Beer on me to celebrate a job well done."

The men headed back to the station that had been built by the volunteers several years prior and put all of their tools and supplies in their proper places. Colin was frequently surprised by how long that took, but knew it was critical so that the next time they were called out, everything would be ready. They met every Saturday morning, though, to go over some exercise, learn something new from the captain and to clean the equipment. But at the rate they were going, there might be another fire before then and they had to be prepared.

"Want to head over to the poblado for aforementioned beer?" James asked as he and Colin locked the door behind them. They were frequently the last to leave, and this time was no different.

"Aye," Colin said, rolling his tongue around the soot that covered his teeth. "I am a bit parched, to be honest with ye."

James nodded, wiping a rag over his beard which was, to Colin's eye, a little grayer than it normally was. The cloth came away more black than white, and they headed across the road.

Colin looked around for a moment outside of the

cantina and scouted the horizon. A large, dark plume had started and he stopped in his tracks, his eye trained on the spot.

"What is it? Smoke?" James stopped too and shielded his eyes from the sun, following Colin's gaze.

The radio clipped to Colin's back pocket hadn't made a sound. He turned it off and back on to make sure he heard the comforting squeak it made—no, there hadn't been a call that they'd missed.

James pointed a bit further to the right. "Look, there's another one."

Colin reached for the binoculars he always carried and looked more closely at both plumes.

He let out a deep breath and shook his head. "No, looks like dust."

"Regular dust devils?" James asked. He turned away from the plumes and held open the door of the cantina, ushering Colin inside.

"No, bigger than normal. With all these fires, I may be a little antsy. But I think it's just dust from riders practicing for the Baja 250."

"Right," James said before they were swallowed up by the cool rush of air and loud laughter inside the cantina. "We'll be over-run with that soon enough. I forgot."

"I did, too. I mean, I love the races, but the hordes of people that come with it I could do without."

James nodded in agreement as the two men crossed through the colorful tables that dotted the restaurant and headed to a table closer to the windows. The cool breeze of the water wafted through there and it was their preferred spot.

Colin looked over at one of the tables in the corner where the old guys held court. They were there every night after they hauled their boats out of the water and cleaned their catch of the day. Empty shot glasses littered the table as they told their fish stories, not many of which could be believed, Colin usually thought. He'd always been friendly with them and he nodded over toward the one he knew best, Bruce, and got a nod in return. Not that it was accompanied with a smile. It was a pretty closed group, and when they weren't talking about fishing, they were moaning about how the south camps had changed and the glory days had gone for good with the new residents and the resort that was in progress.

James and Colin settled into their own regular chairs and nodded as two ice-cold beers appeared in front of them. They walked through the fire again, as they always did, and speculated on how it could have started. By the time the brown bottles were empty, they'd decided they didn't know and were ready to head home. Colin dropped James off with a wave to Megan and headed to his own house on the shore, reliving the fire in his memory once more before he fell into his bed, exhausted.

CHAPTER 3

Hanna had guided her mare back to her house, shaking her head at the encounter with the firefighter. She'd stayed back when she'd first arrived, watching the volunteers do their work. His commanding presence had been comforting at the fire and he certainly knew what he was doing, but after the danger had passed she'd only wanted to help. Why was it no one ever expected horses to be calm and able to handle fire?

As she led Violet into the small corral she'd built when she'd arrived several months ago, she turned to look at where the fire had been but found no sign of flames. Happy that they'd been able to limit any further damage, she made sure the horses had water and slowly walked toward her house.

She plopped down on her patio sofa, gazing at the stars in the night sky. Her thoughts turned to her horses and the years of abuse they had suffered at the hands of cruel ranchers before she had rescued them. She'd learned many things from her mentors about how to treat and train horses in a different way, one of respect and compassion. She'd taken time and care with Violet, and now they were able to almost ride as one. Violet's fear of humans and of fire had subsided, and she was proud of her ability to remain calm and connected to Hanna during any type of situation. Violet still wasn't too sure about the waves and water of the nearby Sea of Cortez, but they could work on that next.

She walked to the refrigerator and grabbed a soda, wondering about how the Irishman had arrived in this small, glorious part of Mexico. She had been surprised by his Irish accent. Here in Baja, that wasn't very common. Spanish accent, yes. Irish, no. She realized she'd like to know more about him, and to show him that her horses could be helpful to the bomberos. They'd suffered greatly and had earned the opportunity.

The pungent odor of smoke still wafted through the air from the fire, and although she'd heeded their request to leave the scene, it was so near to her that she felt as if she was still there. She climbed to the upper patio and leaned against the railing, looking over toward the house that had burned. There was no moon tonight, and while the stars shone brightly, it was very dark. All she could see was what was illuminated by the headlights of the fire trucks—and that wasn't much.

She could see men moving back and forth, and hear some faint voices. She moved a little closer and leaned further over the railing and could make out the voices a little better. She heard the Irish firefighter she'd spoken to—she knew his accent right away—tell her neighbors that he'd come back again tomorrow and take a look. Did that mean he thought there was foul play? She couldn't imagine anyone in the south campos wanting to hurt anyone, and she shook her head, positive it had been an accident.

Her ears perked up when she heard something about the IRA—were they talking about the Irish man? That couldn't be possible, either. She'd known in that brief moment that he was a gentle person. Not just anyone would give so much time to the volunteer firefighters, and she found it hard to believe that he was anything but kind. But maybe if she had the chance, she'd ask him.

Violet whinnied and her other horse, Regalo,

stomped his feet and she realized that she needed to give them another flake of hay before she went to bed. She'd brushed them both earlier in the day and they were really settled for the night, but she liked to give them a little extra on the days that she took them out for a ride.

When she'd first been asked to take Violet and her colt, they'd both been emaciated and had broken free and run from a farm many miles away where they'd both been abused, almost starved to death to boot. She hadn't had the heart to say no—someone had found out that she used to train horses for a living—and in hindsight, it had been one of the best decisions she'd ever made. Sure, they were a lot of work, but they'd taught her to have even more patience than she had before, and confirmed that she was right about the way she wanted to help horses. She used kindness, encouragement and positive reinforcement. It wasn't like she was training them for a rodeo, just trying to teach them how to feel safe with humans again after they'd decided that they'd rather never see a human again in their lives. And she was proud of that.

As she ran her hand down Violet's soft nose, she knew again that she'd been right. Violet had become her friend, and Regalo was now tolerating riders. Big wins on both fronts.

It made her more confident in her decision to move down south, at least part time, to hone her craft of stained glass and continue training horses, although she no longer wanted to do that full time. And while it was quiet down here, she'd made a few friends in the short time she'd been down, and even though she was a bit of a loner, she looked forward to meeting more.

She yawned and stretched, ready for bed after what had been an unexpectedly eventful day. She stood just a bit longer on her patio, closing her eyes with her arms lifted as the cool breeze blew through her hair and she said her thanks for yet another beautiful day.

CHAPTER 4

The sun shone brightly on the water over the Sea of Cortez and Colin whistled an Irish tune as he looked over the beach. Hundreds of birds were diving in a roiling spot in the water, catching their breakfast. The sea was so quiet he could hear their splashes as they swooped in for a feast. It seemed utterly incongruous to the scene the previous evening—the frantic call over the radio, the homeowners in a panic, the firefighters frantically trying to keep everyone safe and contain the fire.

But that was last night. Today, things were definitely more calm, and his thoughts turned to why and how the fire had started in the first place. It wasn't a particularly busy time for tourists—the ones who really didn't know how to live lightly on the seashore—and at this time of year there weren't ordinarily many fires. He was actually looking forward to going back to the fire scene and poking around a little to satisfy his curiosity.

Coffee in hand, he walked further into the warm breeze, sand crunching underfoot. He took a deep breath, the salty air tickling his nostrils, and even though things seemed calm he did what he always did. He shielded his eyes from the sun and looked up the long beach, north to south, searching for smoke. He breathed a bit easier when he saw none.

There were no signs of last night's fire, and he let out a sigh of relief. The fire seemed simple enough, but he couldn't shake a sense that something was off. Was it something about the fire, or seeing a woman on a horse? He'd been in Mexico for five years now and had not heard of any horses, let alone a woman with them. He shook his head started toward the house.

A COMMOTION between his feet let him know that Nala, his border collie, had found him. She scurried between his feet, pausing for a brief moment for a pat on the head. She reminded him of home, of Ireland, as he'd had border collies since he was a small child, walking for miles with them as he helped tend the pastures his father managed.

He thought of his father and their farm that he had left almost five years before. He remembered riding on the back of the fire trucks as they'd rushed to take his father and the other volunteers to work when fires broke out in their community. He'd loved everything about it – the sirens, the danger, the excitement.

When he'd heard the call for volunteer bomberos, as the firefighters in the South Campos where he now lived were called, he had jumped at the chance to participate as a way to honor his father from a far away country. Even if they couldn't be together, they could fight fires together in spirit.

On this calm morning with the sea breeze there were no signs of fire, and he let out a sigh of relief. As he started back toward his house, the black and white dog jumping through the waves grabbed a stick and tossed it toward him, her ears bouncing and her eyes never leaving the piece of wood. He bent over to grab it, tossing it toward the cliff. She bounded to it, bringing it back for another round, tossing it at his feet once more.

"Nala, I can't do this all day with you. You never want to quit." He left the stick where it was and turned inside. "I'll take you for a run on the beach after a while. Right now, we've got work to do."

She followed close behind as he grabbed his keys and headed for the door. He opened the passenger side of the beat-up Jeep with flames painted on the side, and Nala jumped in, her head already hanging out the window.

Returning waves from people as he passed the small hodgepodge of markets and restaurants that made up the center of the South Campos, he replayed the scene of last night's fire in his mind. Although the owner had mentioned fireworks, the house was set back pretty far from the beach, and Colin wasn't convinced that it had been started by errant fireworks. He hadn't been able to make much out in the dark and was eager to see what he could spot today.

He approached the garage slowly from the same direction the engine had come, his eyes moving quickly around the scene. He parked his car a bit away from the charred structure, the acrid smell of burned wood and smoke assaulting his nostrils.

The walls of the garage had been built with the beautiful ladrillo brick common to this area. The mud and clay mixture was fired in tall stacks and was left with patterns of yellow and orange throughout the brick. In construction, they were matched in "whale-tails" and created interesting shapes and patterns through the structure. Now, though, all the sides of the building, inside and out, were black with soot.

He walked toward the building, automatically placing the hard hat on his head that he carried in the car. It appeared that the entire wood roof had been destroyed, but walking into a recently burned structure could always be dangerous and he had learned not to take any chances.

With his boot, he nudged some of the burnt items out of the way and took a peek into the interior. He'd seen the aftermath of many fires, and this one didn't seem particularly unusual. He didn't notice anything obvious that would have started a fire.

"Thanks for coming out again today," he heard from behind him. The owner of the house stood in what had been the opening to the garage.

"Well, you're welcome, but I don't know how much help I can be."

"There's nothing to be done, really, but I appreciate you taking a look around."

"How did you notice the fire? Did you see it start?" Colin picked up a screwdriver that had fallen to the floor and nudged away some more debris.

"My wife and I smelled it before we saw it. Thought maybe someone was having a bonfire on the beach and we always come to check. Saw smoke coming from the roof on the other side and put out the call as fast as we could."

"No explosions of any kind?"

"Well, there was a small initial burst. We probably shouldn't have, but we went inside and grabbed the two extra gas cans and moved them out. There wasn't anything else in there that could have exploded," he said as Colin continued his tour around the sooty building.

"No paint or cleaning supplies of any kind?"

"Oh, that's right. You're a painter, too, aren't you? I'd forgotten. No, nothing like that."

Colin smiled in his direction. "Yes, that's what I do for a living down here. This is just for fun, when the captain lets me."

He rolled up his sleeves and pulled leather gloves on each hand as the owner of the house left him to it. He sifted through the remains inside the garage, systematically moving aside things he'd taken a look at. The camera on his phone clicked quickly as he took pictures of anything he thought might be of value.

An hour later, he knew nothing more than when

he started. He tore off his gloves and his hard hat, throwing them in the back of his Jeep. The irony of the flames he'd painted on the sides wasn't lost on him as he stared back at the fire scene. He'd done it as a joke long ago, before he'd joined the bombers, but now that he drove around the south campos with flames painted on the side of the Jeep, he thought maybe he was more obsessed than was healthy.

Nala jumped as the hard hat clattered against the floor, her nap interrupted. Frustrated, he grabbed the camera he'd brought and turned to take pictures of the scene even though he'd found nothing that could give him a reason for its cause.

The shutter snapped in rapid succession as he quickly took photographs of the damage, hoping he might spot something new and frustrated that he hadn't. As the shutter slowed, he heard a sound behind him that sounded out of place, rhythmic thuds and rapid breathing. His shoulders tensed and he lowered the camera. Turning slowly, he was eye to eye with the beautiful mare from last night. Her head bobbed as if in greeting, and he couldn't help but smile.

Nala jumped out the window of the Jeep and started toward Colin. "Heel, Nala," he said, motioning her over. She sat directly beside him, her eyes trained on the horse in front of her.

"What a beautiful border collie," a female voice said.

Colin's head jerked upward, past the eyes of the horse and onto its rider. The woman from the fire scene sat confidently on her mare, gazing down at Nala, her black hair matching the mane of the beautiful mount and her eyes as deep.

"Oh, thank you. She's a good dog, and I don't expect she'll give your horse any trouble, although she's never seen one before."

The woman's eyes danced and her lips curved into the same smile he'd seen the previous night.

"Never seen a horse before?" Her eyes flickered with laughter. "I find that hard to believe."

"She was born and raised here in Baja, and this is the first horse I've seen in the five years I've lived in Mexico. Well, before last night, anyway. She's not that old." He looked at Nala, whose eyes had not left the horse. "Her name is Nala."

"Ah, a lovely name. Worthy of a border collie."

"Yes, she's a border collie and should be a working dog. Nothing for her to work right now, so she works me. Would have me throwing sticks for her twenty-four hours a day if she could."

The woman's face lit up and she threw her head back, laughing with a sound that he could only think of as the sound of bells.

Colin felt his grin spread as he reached a hand out to pat the horse. "This is a beautiful mare. It's been ages since I've seen a horse. A true sight for sore eyes."

"Oh, you ride?"

"It's been a very long time, but I've been known to once or twice." His eyes met hers now, and he noticed how full of joyful calm they were.

"Well, if you'd like I can take you for a ride. Violet needs to go for a ride tomorrow, and I have another horse that needs to be taken out. Nala can come, too, if you'd like."

He looked up at her, surprised at the offer. "I would love the opportunity. I hope I can remember how."

"It's just like riding a bike. One that eats carrots," she said, laughing at him.

He couldn't help but smile. "I think I have some carrots I can bring."

"Okay, good. Meet me tomorrow at my house," she said, pointing across the arroyo at a brick house with a corral next to it. It had been too dark last night to notice, but it was in plain sight today.

"Violet and I will see you at nine o'clock."

"Okay. Nala and I will be there." Her hair surrounded her face as she turned to ride back over the arroyo, through the ocotillo and cactus. He stood and watched her black hair blow in the breeze, matching that of the mare's tail. It wasn't until she'd entered the arroyo and he couldn't see her that he realized he hadn't asked her name.

CHAPTER 5

The next day dawned warm, the skies clear and the sea calm. Colin threw a quick ice chest together, grabbing the carrots out of the refrigerator, not knowing where he was going or what he was doing today. He'd laughed aloud when he'd realized what he had committed to. He hadn't ridden a horse in years, since he'd left Ireland, and he didn't even know this woman. It could turn out badly, and he wanted at least not to be hungry for it.

It was a beautiful Baja day, the dolphins leaping off shore and traveling south. He marveled at the change in his life since he'd come to Mexico. It had been a big decision for him to leave his family, and Ireland, but he felt he hadn't had a choice.

When he arrived, he knew he stuck out like a

sore thumb. His wavy, reddish brown hair and green eyes gave him away as a foreigner among the locals, most with dark hair and dark eyes. His height also gave him away. At six foot two, he was tall and muscular, towering over the majority of the men who lived in the poblado, the small group of houses that was the closest thing to a town within many miles. But his easy laugh and outgoing manner had helped him make many friends, and he felt he was a bit more accepted now. He'd made a point of learning to speak Spanish as quickly as he could, and it had made all the difference in the world.

He wondered about this woman on the horse as he drove over the ruts and rocks on the road toward her campo. Her beauty and serenity had captured his attention, and her instinctive manner with her mare was intriguing. As he turned down the dirt road into her campo, he stopped wondering how he had never met or noticed her before. It wasn't as if he could ask anybody about her. He still didn't know her name.

He drove up in the half-circle drive, pulling up to her front door. Her house was beautiful, and from her back patio, you could walk straight onto the beach. The front door was made of heavy, dark wood with horses etched on it. In the center was the most beautiful piece of stained glass he had ever seen. The sun shone into the back of the house and through the glass, lighting up the turquoise, crimson, purple and yellow of the design as if it were in a church.

From inside he heard a tune, a lilting voice, not high and not low. He thought it sounded very serene and he recognized the Mexican song as an old one that he had heard the mariachi's sing in town.

Gingerly knocking on the side of the door, he avoided the stained glass. It swung open and she stood there, about shoulder height to him. Her shiny black hair was pulled in a ponytail, and her white Mexican top with colorful embroidery framed her face over her riding jeans. Today, her riding boots were red, matching the baseball cap she wore.

"You're right on time," she said, turning away from the door and heading back into the kitchen. "I'm almost ready. Packing a picnic."

"I brought some things as well." He followed her lead into the kitchen and set his knapsack on the beautiful blue tile counter.

"Great. I love to eat. The more the merrier." She laughed, pouring a cup of coffee for him.

"I didn't catch your name yesterday. Or the night before." He took the cup she offered and watched her over the rim of the mug as he took a sip.

"I don't believe I told you. My name is Hanna. Hanna Johnson."

"Colin Stewart," he said, setting the mug on the counter and offering her his hand.

She took it and, with a firm shake, said, "I know who you are. Everybody knows who you are."

His eyebrows shot up and he felt his stomach clench. He'd taken care to keep a low profile.

"What do you mean? I'm just a painter."

"Painter by day, bombero by night," she laughed, her eyes lighting up. "You have quite a reputation with fire."

"I just like to help," he said, the knot in his stomach easing. "I really don't want to be famous. Or infamous."

"Low profile, huh? Me, too." She set the empty mugs in the sink and threw the knapsack over her shoulder. "I've already saddled Violet and Regalo. Are you ready to go?"

"Regalo? Doesn't that mean gift in Spanish?"

"Yes, it does. He was a special gift to me and so I chose that name for him."

"I can't promise a stellar riding performance. It's been a long time for me, but I'm willing to try." He opened the car door for Nala and she bounded out after him.

"My horses are special, and I think you'll find it an easy, fun experience." She winked at him and he hoped she was right.

He was grateful that Hanna had already saddled up the horses as his memory was a little fuzzy about how to do it. Regalo was a big horse, almost sixteen hands tall, and even at Colin's height he had to try a couple of times to hop on him. The saddle she had chosen was sturdy, and he felt confident that he would have a good ride.

Hanna placed the knapsacks in the saddlebags and jumped on Violet with a graceful hop. She looked natural in the saddle, almost as if she was more comfortable riding than walking.

She headed out on the beach, Colin following and Nala bringing up the rear. The waves played against the sand as the tide came in and shells covered the sand beneath them. They fell into a comfortable silence for a bit as the breeze worked against them.

Hanna and Violet turned up an arroyo and headed toward the desert. Away from the beach, the wind died down and it was warm and quiet.

"Where are we headed?" Colin asked, pulling up alongside Hanna. Nala wasn't quite sure what to do with this move and ran back and forth behind the two horses, wanting to herd them. They both laughed as they watched Nala try to be in charge. Both horses just snorted at her.

"I thought we'd head up to the fossil mounds. It's not too far and we can have lunch there. Have you been?"

"No, I haven't, but I've heard about them. Do you know the story?"

"Yes. They are shell remains from the sea that have been in these huge mounds so long that they've become fossilized. They look like rocks now in the shape of seashells. They are beautiful."

"How did they get there?" he asked, his eyebrows raised in curiosity.

"They are ancient places where the native people lived long ago. They survived mostly on shellfish and left the shells."

"Are you native?" He again noticed her long, dark hair and brown eyes. She looked as if she could be.

"I have native blood deep in my ancestry, yes," she answered, guiding her horse down a worn path toward the mountains. "I have studied native traditions, especially as it relates to horses. I find their methods to be...kind. Instinctive, and more respectful of the horse than our western ways."

"What do you mean?" he asked, thinking of the

way horses were trained in Ireland, at least on his farm, with the harnesses and whips they'd used. He'd never thought there could be another method, and had spent many hours trying to break in young colts under his father's watchful eye.

"I believe that all creatures should be treated with respect, with dignity. And rather than bending them to your will, you can make them your partners, so that they want to do you what bid them to do."

He peered at her from under the brim of his hat. Her eyes were straight forward on the horizon, and her lips were curved in a smile. It looked to him as if she and Violet were walking in unison, not one riding the other, and he wondered if she could be right.

CHAPTER 6

The rattle came from behind Nala as she walked along behind the horses. Colin and Hanna's heads spun at the same moment toward the sound that he recognized as a rattlesnake. As Colin turned, he pulled the reins hard and Regalo reared back a bit, taking off like a shot down the road ahead.

Colin held on tightly, eyes narrowed, trying to remember everything he knew about riding. He pulled back on the reins and turned to see Nala bounding behind him, Hanna following quickly. His heart raced as he regained control and finally pulled the horse to a stop.

Colin's heart beat quickly as he patted Regalo's

neck, both of their breathing slowly returning to normal.

"That sounded like a pretty big rattlesnake. I can't ever get used to them. There aren't snakes in Ireland, don't you know, and I'm not the best with 'em." He knew from her smile that he must have looked a sight with the horse taking off like that.

"Regalo wouldn't have done that if he hadn't felt your fear."

"I wasn't afraid. Just surprised." His jaw hardened and his chin jutted out as he leveled his eyes at her.

Her eyebrows inched upward as she said, "Suit yourself. But my horses are trained to be in tune with their rider. They take your emotional lead rather than the lead of the reins."

"I'm not sure what you mean. I pulled his reins and he stopped."

"Yes, but not because you pulled on his reins; because you were ready to stop. No longer panicked."

"I wasn't panicked." He heard his voice harden a bit. Who was this girl to tell him what he was feeling, anyway?

"Okay. I understand," she said and eased Violet to her left, walking further on the creek bed toward the mountains. "We're almost there. Follow me."

"What do you mean, you understand?" he said quietly, but she had already gone ahead of him. He urged Regalo to keep up, and they galloped up ahead and around a curve. Hanna had stopped in front of what looked like a huge sand dune with specks of white in it.

She turned as he came up, smiling. "This is it."

He dismounted, looping Regalo's reins over the branch of a nearby elephant tree. Spotting Nala, he motioned to her to follow him as they walked toward the mound.

Hanna secured Violet and followed slowly, with an air of reverence as she approached the mound.

"My ancestors lived here for centuries before they abandoned the spot. This is where they lived, fed their families, made a life."

"How did they survive? It's so hot here in the summer."

"They lived with the rhythm of the seasons, but fished and clammed all year round. In the winter, they lived here, closer to the mountains. They hunted abundant deer, rabbits and other small animals. Probably snakes, too," she said, and quickly glanced at him, her eyes flickering.

"Too bad they didn't get them all." With a quick glance around, he returned her smile.

"Doesn't seem like you'd have survived as a native." She motioned to him as she moved closer to the mound. Kneeling down, she picked up what looked like a rock and handed it to him.

The rock looked like a perfectly formed clam, closed as if it had just been found in the sea. It was heavier, though, as it had turned to stone. He was amazed by its beauty, and holding it in his hand, he felt the warm breeze touch his face and heard the elephant trees rustle.

"Did you feel that?" he asked her, turning the fossil over in his hand.

"Yes. There is much you can feel here, if you are willing. I believe the spirits dwell here, even now."

He turned to her and his mouth opened, as if to speak. He looked from the fossil to her, and felt as if he'd been thrown back in time, sensing the importance of where he was. His pulse quickened, and an ancient scene of her with her horse, at this place flashed through his mind.

He shook his head and moved closer to the mound himself. Picking up another stone, he said, "What is this one?"

She moved to where he was, her hand outstretched. As she took the stone from his hand, the breeze moved again, almost in a circle around them, throwing dirt in the air surrounding them. They both looked up as the horses whinnied by the trees.

"That was strange," he said as the breeze died as quickly as it had come up.

"I don't think so," she said, smiling at him. "The spirits speak here in many ways."

"Well, if that's the spirits speaking, I'm not sure I want to know what they have to say," he laughed, turning back to the mound. He pointed to her hand and said, "What is that one?"

"This is a fossilized scorpion."

"So these Indians survived on wild game and catches from the sea?"

"Yes, in addition to grinding mesquite flour. Mesquite trees were plentiful at that time, but have mostly been used for firewood since. There are petroglyphs in the mountains depicting more of what I'm describing." She turned and walked toward the horses. "I'm going to give the horses some water if you'd like to lay out lunch."

He caught the knapsacks as she tossed them to him and grabbed the blanket he had put in Regalo's saddlebags. Under the shade of a salt cedar tree, he laid out the blanket and dug into the knapsacks.

She had packed a Mexican meal, complete with

freshly made salsa, beans, rice and avocados. As he took a wrapped package from the bag, he lifted it to his nose, inhaling the wonderful aroma of the warm, round tortillas.

"Yes, they are homemade," she said, surprising him from close behind.

"You make your own tortillas?" he said, not able to hide his admiration.

She sat down on the blanket beside him and set down two bottles of Indio, Mexico's best dark beer and his favorite.

"Yes, my grandmother taught me. There's no comparison, in my opinion, and I prefer to make them myself."

He quickly filled two tortillas with beans, rice, salsa and avocado, handing her one and biting into the other.

"Be careful, my salsa is—"

He coughed as the heat of the jalapenos seared his tongue. Sputtering, he grabbed for the bottle and took a big swig of Indio.

Her laughter danced in the arroyo as he wiped the sweat from his eyes and tried to catch his breath. "I was going to warn you."

"Guess I didn't give you a chance." He felt the color coming back into his face.

"Are you all right?"

His face now beet red, he said, "Yes, absolutely. I love it spicy."

"You could have fooled me. I thought you were going to choke."

"Ah, it's a pleasurable pain, lass. The hotter the better."

"More, then?" she said as she made another taco and held it out to him."

"Oh, yes, please." As he took the food from her hand, he met her gaze. She quickly dropped her eyes toward the blanket, smiling.

"I'm glad you like it," she said quietly.

After they'd eaten, Hanna quickly packed up and tossed everything they'd brought with them into the saddlebags. He watched her do it with speed, grace and efficiency and only turned away when she caught him watching. But if he'd had his way, he'd be happy watching her do anything at all. Even pull weeds if he got to see the wind toss her hair around and the sparkle in her eyes when she looked out over the horizon.

Just as they were ready to head back to the beach, she turned toward the mound and closed her eyes, raised her arms and said, "Thank you."

She turned to him and smiled, which made him smile even bigger.

"You ready to go?" she asked as she untied the horses from the small tree. She waited for him to nod. "Follow me."

Even though he'd only known her a few days, there was something about her that made him pretty positive he'd follow her just about anywhere.

CHAPTER 7

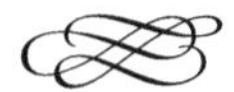

"Were you raised here in Mexico?" he asked as they started the ride back down the arroyo and toward the beach.

"No, I wasn't. I was born and raised in San Diego, but was very much steeped in the traditions of my culture, both Spanish and native. I have many relatives here in Baja, and I spent much time here as a child."

"I haven't seen you here before."

"After I graduated from college, I went on to study horses and began to train them with the ancient methods. Many people didn't understand what I was trying to do, so I decided to move down here and train in a quieter environment. I did that for years. Until I wanted to stop."

Colin pulled Regalo beside Violet as the narrow dirt road widened into the arrow. He glanced at her, wanting to know more.

"Why did you want to stop?"

She pushed her hat back on her head and wiped her brow with her forearm, her eyes straight ahead. After a moment of silence, she turned to look at him, her brown eyes soft.

"I understand that there are different methods for all kinds of things, but the places I was finding needed horse trainers did things much differently than I wanted to."

"Oh," Colin said. He leaned forward and stroked Regalo's mane. He certainly was a gentle horse, and Hanna had done a great job with him. "You certainly do know what you're doing. Regalo is quite the gentleman."

Hanna laughed and looked fondly at Regalo. "Well, if you'd seen him when he was gifted to me, you wouldn't have said that."

Colin frowned and looked down at the handsome horse. He'd taken good care of his rider and once Colin had gotten his riding legs back, they'd ridden as if a team.

"What do you mean? You didn't have him from the beginning?"

She shook her head slowly, slowing down to watch an osprey cross the sky on its way to the sea to hunt, its baby close behind.

"No. When I got him, he and Violet had been beaten almost to death. She'd been chained for months a long time, forced to breed on a farm. When Regalo was born and strong enough, he attacked the farmers and Violet did the same. They turned them loose in the desert."

"Oh, no," Colin said, the image almost too painful to think of.

"I don't know why they didn't kill them. It was almost as if they wanted to torture them even more, leaving them to starve. Some people found them near death on the side of the road and brought them to me."

Colin hung his head for a moment, pained by the thought.

"You've done a remarkable thing here, Hanna," he said quietly. "They seem very happy, and you saved their lives."

Her smile was back when she turned to him again. "Yes, things worked out well after a very, very long time. I had to be patient and consistent. And kind. And just wait."

They rode a bit further and Colin rolled that all

over in his mind—the commitment and love it must have taken to do that day in and day out with horses you didn't know and who certainly didn't want to have anything to do with you.

"So you hadn't expected this when you moved south. You're kind of young to be down here with all the misfits," he said with a laugh.

She nodded. "I thought that myself for a while. But after I decided I couldn't train horses in California, I just came down here to kind of decide what I did want to do. I had started a business creating stained glass, and I can do that down here also. It's perfect for me, and I don't see people that often."

"That would explain why I haven't seen you. Maybe it would be good for you to meet more people."

She glanced at him quickly. "I'm not sure I want to, honestly. I like my solitude. I'm not sure why I even asked you to join me today except that I needed another rider for Regalo."

"Thanks, a lot." He laughed, and he saw her lips turn up in a smile under the brim of her hat. "Well, if you would like to meet more people, tomorrow is the annual Firefighter's Fundraiser if you'd like to come. We're doing a demonstration for the kids with the fire truck and there's a band and barbecue. I think they're also having an auction."

She didn't respond, her eyes fixed on the horizon.

"Hello? Hanna?"

"Sh," she said quickly, raising her finger to her lips. "I see something." She pointed to an area a few hundred yards ahead and off to the right, partially hidden by a dune.

An old shack sat set back from the creek bed. Smoke came from a metal chimney sticking out the back.

"That doesn't smell very good," she said. "What is it?"

"Well, it's not carne asada, that's for sure. Barbecued beef in Mexico smells really good, and that's not it. Smells like chemicals to me."

"I don't see any cars there, do you?" Her eyes drifted over the landscape of ocotillo and elephant trees toward the run-down shack.

"I think we should take a look," he said as he urged Regalo toward the smoke.

They rode on in silence for a bit, watching the shack closely as they passed and noticing that the smoke changed color from black to white as they rode by. "Does that car look familiar?" Hanna asked.

"No, not to me," he said, he said, looking over the

aging blue Jeep. "But the smell does, sort of. I can't quite pin it. But looks at least to be under control."

They passed the shed and Colin slowed down, looking around the shed for anything that looked unusual. There were lots of sheds back in the desert where people lived for various and sundry reasons—mostly because they just wanted to be alone. He shook his head and decided that it really wasn't any of his business and as they reached the beach, he galloped a bit to catch up with her. "What about the fundraiser tomorrow?" he asked again.

She looked up at him quickly, as if startled. "Oh. We'll see," she said, turning forward as they reached her home on the beach.

CHAPTER 8

The old fire engine creaked as Colin closed the compartment's door, the water hose wound tightly inside. He wiped one more spot off the shiny red paint and stepped back, admiring his work. The truck sparkled and he smiled, feeling ready for the day's events.

"You all ready for the show today?" he heard from behind him, followed by a smack on the shoulder. "Looks nice, Colin. Well done."

His friend, James, smiled with him as they admired the engine, the red paint gleaming in the sun.

"She's a beauty on the outside, even if a bit unpredictable on the inside," he proudly said.

"I know you were a tad worried that we wouldn't

be able to pull this off today. The annual fundraiser, and the fire truck not working? Maybe we could have raised more money if they'd known we'd be responding to a house fire on bicycles carrying buckets." James's eyes twinkled as he teased his friend.

"I wasn't going to let that happen. Took me five days to find the part and another three to fix it, but we're running," Colin said, polishing yet one more streak off the engine he'd just washed. "Besides, we're the only people around from across the pond. Needed to show them what we're made of, eh?

James laughed and joined Colin in wiping off the final streaks left by washing the truck. "Who'd ever have thought that an Irishman and Englishman would be doing this together on the beach in Mexico?"

"Certainly not me," Colin said as he stood back once more and proclaimed the truck ready to go. "Everyone's still shocked that we've become friends, since they all seem to think I'm an ex-IRA member and you're a British spy."

James's laugh echoed through the station as he doubled over. "Most ridiculous thing I've heard. It seems it's a rumor that just won't die. Megan still isn't sure I've told her the truth. Thinks I might be James Bond in hiding."

"Why would she think otherwise after your capture of the smugglers last month? And even of the man behind it. If you told me you were a spy, I'd believe you," he teased.

"You know that was just a coincidence. But glad I was able to help, after all. Meeting Megan was an extra bonus."

"And I'm not able to convince people I've nothing to do with the IRA either," he said. "No matter what I say, people just look at me and smile."

"Well, let's give them a real show today, then. It'll probably convince them for sure that the rumors are true and we'll never be able to tell them otherwise."

The old joke had been around for years, and neither one of them worked too hard to convince people it wasn't true. They'd become fast friends and frequently laughed over it.

"Time to go, mate," James said as he gathered the rags. "The other guys are here and I'm sure all the kids are waiting for us."

"I bet they're sure eager to sit in the truck, as they are every year."

"Yeah, just like you were as a lad," James reminded him. Colin had shared his childhood stories with James as they'd spent time after fire calls sipping tequila and chatting. Colin had shared that he'd grown up in Ireland helping his father fight fires and that had inspired Colin's commitment to doing the same in their new home and community.

Grabbing the keys and hopping in the truck, he turned the engine over, grateful that it sputtered to life. The equipment they had to work with was old and unreliable, and the event today was the major source of funding for the year. He was pleased that the demonstration would go on, hopefully without a hitch, and that the coffers of the volunteer firefighters would be full for another year.

He waved at James as he backed the fire truck out of the small fire station. Spying his hair in the rearview mirror, he swore under his breath at its refusal to stay in place. Grabbing his hat, he smiled at the word, "Bomberos" embroidered on it and pulled it on his head, shoving a lock of his wavy hair underneath.

Living on the beach, in Playa Luna, was never something he'd have guessed would be his reality. He had come from Ireland, and looked glaringly different than the locals. His reddish-brown hair and green eyes pegged him as a foreigner almost everywhere he went, and when he'd first arrived, he hadn't been sure he'd ever be able to fit in.

As he joined his fellow firefighters gearing up for the demonstration, he realized he finally felt at home. He was looking forward to the fundraiser and was proud that he could be part of it.

Joining the bomberos, the volunteer firefighters in this remote area, had been one of the things that had made him the happiest. It felt familiar to him, and he enjoyed helping the community.

His father had been a volunteer firefighter in Ireland, and he'd often been taken along as a child. He hadn't wanted to leave Ireland, and the fond memories of his family, his homeland, remained as he tried to integrate into the community and culture of the beach, of Mexico, that he now called home.

The excitement he had felt lingered even now, and when he'd moved here and the call came out for volunteers, he had signed on immediately.

"Everybody's here but Robert," James said as he guided Colin out of the garage and down the dirt road toward the day's events.

"He let me know on the radio that he'd be late," Colin replied. "Something to do in town."

Colin stopped briefly as the firefighters, in full fire suits, hopped on the truck. The demonstration was planned for just beside the fundraiser. Colin spotted the multi-colored tents full of spectators and saw all of the young kids lined up on the path leading in. He grinned as he flipped the lights and siren on and headed toward the show.

Loud whistles and clapping from the crowd rose even over the sound of the siren. Colin grinned as he pulled the fire truck up next to a set of tires that had been set on fire earlier by his captain, especially for the demonstration. His crew-mates jumped off the engine, expertly opening the compartments holding their equipment. As they ran toward the fire with hoses in tow, the children jumped up and down, screaming in excitement.

The adults standing behind them were just as amused, having been fueled with margaritas, beer and wine as they waited for the bomberos and enjoyed the band.

As Colin watched the crew, he was thankful the day was beautiful and not too hot for the crew to run around in full gear. He smiled as it all went off without a hitch, hoping that the coffers would fill and they would raise enough to buy some much-needed first aid equipment. You never knew when an accident would occur, either motorcyclers on the beach or motorhome travelers on the main highway. He wanted to be ready for anything.

He glanced around the crowd and spotted Hanna standing under one of the tents. Surprised, his gaze lingered, and he was captivated by her colorful Mexican skirt and flowing top. As her eyes met his, he thought he noticed her blush.

The final flames were contained, and as the crowd continued to applaud, the children were allowed to see the fire truck up close. Young boys were fascinated with the bomberos' gear and all reached out to touch the shiny yellow suits.

As the cheers died and the children moved back toward the desserts, the firefighters were able to share high-fives all around. Colin was pleased, and started to remove his gear to put it in the truck.

"That was quite an impressive display," he heard from behind him as he placed the last of his gear inside the compartment. He turned quickly, and Hanna's colorful skirt swirled as the wind blew across from the sea.

His smile widened as he said, "Glad you liked it, ma'am." Tipping his hat, he gave a slight not in her direction. "I'm very glad you came. Are you enjoying the fiesta?"

"I've never seen anything quite like it. These

people sure do love you guys, and the kids were a hoot to watch."

"It's one of those events that seems to bring everybody out," he said, glancing around the crowd. "Even some of the more eccentric characters." He nodded his head slight to the left, pointing his thumb in that direction toward a group of older men hoisting beers and singing loudly.

"Who are they?" she asked, her hand over her mouth hiding a smile.

He turned to look at the group of older gentlemen, the old guard of the South Campos. "Well, they will tell you that they are the original pioneers of this area. They've been coming since the mid-sixties, some of them. They started with shacks on the beach and left their wives at home. Still do, I think. That way, they don't ever have to take showers," he said, his eyes twinkling with laughter.

"Oh, the fishing guys," she said. "I overheard them talking about how much has changed and it sounds like they're not too happy about the resort going in up at Rancho del Sol."

"Aw, they'll be all right. Always something to complain about. The resort is being planned well and will help out the whole area. They've just got to complain about something," he said, noticing that the laughter had died a bit and one of the men was looking at him intently. Their eyes met, and the gentleman looked quickly away.

"Who was that?" she said. "He didn't seem to like you too much."

"Aw, that's old Bruce. He's the most outspoken against the resort and has been coming the longest. He's harmless ... but usually could use a shower," he said as he turned back to Hanna. "Let's get something to eat."

As he held out his hand, gesturing for Hanna to lead the way, he lost his balance as the ground shook beneath him. His arms flew around Hanna as the quiet was shattered with the sound of an explosion. The sound of the Rolling Stone's "It's Just a Shot Away" stopped mid-verse as the band fell silent. All eyes turned toward the sound of the explosion and Colin's heart raced as he spied a huge, black plume of smoke coming from one of the campos to the north.

BOOM! Colin almost lost his balance as another explosion ripped through the air. "Are you all right?" he said to Hanna, his ears ringing.

"Yes, I'm fine. Go." She squeezed his hand, her eyes anxious.

As he headed toward the engine, his crew also

turned from the sound of the blast, heading back toward the truck. Quickly, they slipped their arms and legs into the fire suits they'd just removed. Without a word, they all took their places on the truck as Colin once again turned over the engine, heading toward the plumes of smoke. There was no need for the lights or sirens this time. With the entire community at the fundraiser, no one would be on the road between them and the raging fire.

CHAPTER 9

Hanna watched as the fire engine disappeared toward the fire, sending a plume of dust in its wake. It had all happened so suddenly, she wasn't sure what to think. One minute, they'd all been applauding the demonstration, dancing to the music, and the next it was all over. She'd been looking forward to the day, but her stomach knotted at the thought of the homeowners in danger.

A woman from the crowd came up to her and introduced herself as Megan.

"It's hard when they leave in a hurry, and you never know how dangerous it's going to be."

Hanna paused for a moment, not sure what the woman was talking about. She was a little older, and lovely. Her blonde hair blew about in the breeze, and she looked peaceful. Happy. Like Hanna wanted to be.

"I know you like him," she teased as they both watched Colin and James race off toward the fire. "James and I haven't been together all that long, but he trusts Colin with his life. That I do know.

"I haven't been here all that long, either. It's nice to meet someone local. I didn't realize how isolated I'd be here. Mostly, that's okay with me, but it's very nice to meet you," Hanna said, a small smile creeping across her face.

They both watched the fire engine disappear into the distance.

"He's incredibly handsome. And that accent! I thought James's British accent was great, but Irish?"

Hanna changed the subject. "He's very handsome, but a little, um, goofy."

"Goofy? That's the last word I'd use to describe him. He's a great painter, always busy, and takes his work with the bomberos very seriously."

"It seems that way," Hanna said, her eyes on the plumes of smoke in the distance. "Should we go try to help?"

"James always tells me that more people equals

more trouble. Best to let them handle it. If it's a big fire and they need help, they'll call on the radio."

Megan left to go help tear down the tents, and Hanna followed, pulling her eyes away from the smoke, surprised that her heart was beating so quickly.

Hanna and Megan chatted while they helped tear down the tents and put everything away as the crowd dwindled. It was a clearly a disappointment to everyone, but also a compliment that they hadn't wanted to continue without the bomberos present—the entire event was in their honor.

As people headed to their cars, Hanna did notice that they were dropping money into the collection jar, and she knew Colin would be pleased about that.

It was all she could do to focus on her task at hand. With relief, Megan peppered her with questions about her horses and her training methods, and she was able to take her mind off of the fire, wondering if Colin was all right.

After she'd answered as many questions as Megan could muster, she asked, "Don't you ever worry when they go to fight a fire?"

Megan stopped and stared out to the sea for a moment before she responded. "Yes. All the time. I don't suppose you ever stop worrying, but you do get better at keeping busy until they come back, safe and sound."

At this moment, Hanna couldn't imagine ever being able to do that, and she held her hand to her chest as her heart continued to beat faster than she could remember it having done before.

CHAPTER 10

"Hey, Colin, take it easy," James said as his hands flew out to grab onto the side of the cab, his head bouncing off the ceiling.

"This is serious, James. Sorry," Colin replied as his eyes narrowed and he tried to spot the right road to turn onto off the main highway.

"I know, but I'd like to get there without being knocked unconscious."

The radio in the truck crackled on as they searched for information about which campo they were heading to. The blue backdrop of the water on the horizon made the black plumes look even more menacing as they neared the scene.

"I can't quite get a good look at it. There seems to

be something in front of it, or maybe it's down in an arroyo."

"Bomberos, bomberos! Fire at Campo Playa Luna, north arroyo," shouted a voice over the marine radio.

James gripped the seat more tightly, his knuckles even whiter. "That's my camp."

Colin looked over at him and saw the blood drain from his face.

"Hurry," James said. "If it's in the north arroyo, it's trouble. All the houses down there are stick-built, all wood. No ladrillo brick homes and they could go up fast."

The hurried down the road to Playa Luna, following the plumes of smoke as the engine bumped over the ruts. The arroyo came into view and Colin breathed a loud sigh of relief.

"Looks like just one house at the moment. Let's see if we can keep it that way."

Colin pulled the engine close to the fire, careful to keep a bit of distance between the flames and the gasoline in the truck. James and the other crew got out the water hoses, one from each side of the truck and attacked the flames from opposite directions, protecting the houses on each side.

As Colin led the other crew up toward the house, Jimmy Martin, the oldest resident of the camp, raced up on his quad, skidding to stop in the sand behind the fire truck.

"Need any help?" he asked Colin.

"Whose house is this?" Colin said quickly, motioning for the crew to go ahead of him.

"It's Karen and Mike's. They're not here right now. He's a fireman in California," Jimmy said with a straight face.

"Well, that's not going to help him now. How many propane tanks?"

"One that I know of, and it already exploded."

Colin's biggest concern in house fires in the South Campos was the propane tanks. The all-solar houses were efficient with electricity, but all homes relied on propane for heating and cooking. It was most common that the propane tanks exploding was what started the fires the bomberos responded to.

"If you could help keep people away unless they have hoses, that would be great," Colin shouted as he moved toward the fire with his crew.

Whiskers, Jimmy's scruffy terrier, barked at the firefighters or the fire. Colin couldn't quite tell which.

"We're on it," Jimmy muttered as he hurried around to the back side of the houses, up the cliff of the arroyo, Whiskers close behind. As Colin started to knock down the door with his ax, he saw Jimmy on the cliff organizing the hose and bucket brigade.

They'd made a bit of progress before the captain's truck rolled to a stop beside the smoldering house.

"We tried to follow with the second water truck but it wouldn't start," a young man said as the newest bombero jumped out of the captain's truck.

The captain got out more slowly, pausing for a moment to survey the smoldering remains of the house in front of him. His hands clenched into fists as he walked toward Colin, James and the crew as they sat and caught their breath.

"Well, looks like we were lucky again," the captain said as he kicked some debris into a pile. "Did this get all the way over here from the explosion?"

Colin shook his head. "We're just not sure, Captain. We found the propane tank that exploded, but not sure what made it explode in the first place."

"One propane tank? Not two," the captain said, his eyes narrowing. "I think we all heard two explosions from the fundraiser."

James took his helmet off and poured a bottle of water over his head, wiping away the remaining sweat with a rag. "We were just talking about that,

Captain. I mean, we're all amateurs here, but we know what we heard."

Sitting down on the brick wall next to the crew, the captain said, "Colin, did you find anything suspicious at the fire scene the other night? In the small garage?"

"I'm not an expert here, but I didn't see anything obvious."

"No gas, propellants, anything like that?"

Colin wondered what the captain was getting at. He was a retired fire captain from the United States and had come to live in the south campos permanently, responsible in large part for creating the bomberos and securing their equipment, aged and unpredictable as it was. Colin had learned a lot from him and considered him a friend.

"The homeowner said they'd removed the gas cans, and I didn't find anything I could recognize. I did take pictures, but haven't looked at them yet. Do you suspect something?"

"At this point, no, but two fires in three days almost tops all the fires we've had in the past year. Fires are supposed to be rare events, and lately they haven't been."

"Who would light fires on purpose?" Robert, the

young man who'd arrived with the captain, said as his voice raised an octave. "That's just wrong."

James shrugged his shoulders. "Who knows? Don't know who would smuggle fish or drugs or steal land either. Not my kind of people, that's for sure."

Robert stared at the embers, his eyes wide. "I know I'm kind of new here, but I heard there were some undercover spies and IRA bombers living down here. Maybe they did it."

James and Colin looked at each other and burst out laughing. James fell off the brick wall flat onto the sand. Colin reached out his hand, pulling him upright as he laughed as well.

"You're looking at 'em, son," the captain said with a wide grin. "That's the rumor, anyway."

"Don't believe everything you hear, Robert. We're just working men who live on the beach and like tequila every once in a while. No conspiracy at hand."

Colin's face reddened as he turned away and headed toward the captain's car.

"He'll learn, gentlemen," the captain said. "He was a volunteer in the states but got in a little trouble. My sister asked me to look after him for a bit. He's a handful." He rolled his eyes as he followed Colin back to the car. "Meet you at the station. Nice work."

As the captain drove away from the scene, James said, "Want to take a peek inside? Looks like it's cooled down enough." He tossed Colin his helmet while he placed his own back on.

"All right. Maybe we can see something this time. Didn't have much luck last time."

"It's probably nothing. The captain's just thinking it through, I'm sure. Might as well check while we're still here and suited up."

The crew had sorted the engine out and coiled the hoses, all equipment placed back in perfect order by the time James and Colin came out of the house.

"Find anything in there?" Javier said. "We know about the one propane tank, but anything else?"

"Not sure," Colin said. "I'm going to call Mike and ask him if he had any metal five-gallon drums. I didn't think he had, last time I was down to visit. But there's one in there."

"Probably had old oil in there if I know him," James said. "We should ask, though, and let the captain know."

The men moved slowly as they climbed on the truck for the ride back to the station.

James leaned his head against the window of the

cab. "Well, today sure didn't turn out the way I thought it would. Didn't even get to eat at the fundraiser."

Colin frowned as he thought of all the people at the fundraiser, the wasted food and raffle prizes.

No, and I didn't get to dance with Hanna. Colin turned the engine onto the main road and headed toward the station.

CHAPTER 11

A tennis ball square in the forehead woke Colin with a start as the sun streamed in his bedroom window. Nala stood over him, panting loudly and eyeing the ball she'd just dropped. He grimaced, grabbing a paper towel and wiping off his face before turning and throwing the ball as far toward the water as he could. Even as an everyday occurrence, Nala's "wake-up" ritual always surprised him.

He poured water in the coffee pot, hoping a strong cup would jar him awake. His muscles ached after the past two days. Riding a horse and fire fighting this frequently were more than he was used to.

As the fog lifted, he went back over the last fire

scene in his head. They'd done everything right, as far as he knew, and was glad only the one house had been destroyed. But his memory kept skipping over the two explosions. Only one propane tank but two explosions didn't make any sense to him.

He poured himself a cup of coffee and sat down at his kitchen table. Looking over the ocean and mesmerized by the waves, he glanced at the clock and realized he was late for his painting job. Quickly feeding Nala and shrugging on his painter's pants, he loaded his supplies in the Jeep and headed out, Nala riding shotgun.

He turned down the road to his job site and realized with a start that it was in Hanna's campo. He slowed a bit as he passed her house, wondering what she was doing. Regalo and Violet stomped their feet and neighed as Nala barked when they passed. He made a mental note to stop and see her after he'd finished painting for the day. The sight of her at the fundraiser hadn't left his mind, and he shook his head trying to clear it for the task at hand. He was behind schedule painting this mural and wanted to keep his word to the homeowner. *Focus, Colin.*

He set out his paints and stood back for a moment to look at the mural he'd been working on. The circular shape on the side of a house was exactly what the owner had commissioned. He enjoyed painting ocean murals, and had taken great care to get the scale of the dolphins jumping out of the water just right. The intense colors of the ocean, the blues and whites that he had used, stood in contrast with the white of the background and the yellow, pinks and purples of the seashells in the foreground. He nodded, happy with the way it was turning out and set about finishing.

He'd been painting for an hour or two before standing back to assess his progress. He rubbed his hands as they cramped, placing his brushes in lacquer thinner to clean them. He'd brought a big can of it as he knew he'd be changing colors frequently today.

Intently focusing on his work, his head jerked up as he heard a female voice say, "That's beautiful." Hanna stood behind him, hands on her hips as she admired the mural. "Seems you're a man of many talents."

"I don't know if I'd say talent, but I do love to do it."

"Like me and my stained glass," she said, moving closer to the mural to get a better look.

"You do that stained glass? The ones that are your house?" he said, his mouth falling open.

Her laugh lilted through the air like bells, he thought. "Yes, I do. I'm still learning, but, like you, I love to do it."

"I'm very impressed." He turned back to his brushes as he noticed his palms start to sweat.

"I don't consider myself an artist, I just do it for a hobby," she said, turning back toward him.

"Don't say that. What you do is art, and I'll challenge any man who says otherwise." His eyes lit up and he felt he actually would.

"Thank you for defending my honor, sir," she laughed. "Even if as an artist." Color rose in her cheeks as she looked away.

"What are you cleaning your brushes in?" she said. "It smells awful."

"Ah, in my world, the smell of lacquer and linseed oil are akin to the aroma of fresh-baked bread."

"Ugh. I can't imagine," she said, crinkling her nose.

"You just don't know what you're missing," he laughed. "Highly flammable, though. I try to use it only in open spaces."

"Well, it doesn't get much more open than this." She held her arms up toward the sea, her eyes closed and head bowed. The warm breeze sending her hair billowing once again.

"No, it doesn't," he replied, staring at her as she bowed toward the sea.

"What was that for?" he asked, a bit confused at the action.

"I have profound respect for the sea, for its inhabitants, and for nature in general. Sometimes I get overwhelmed with gratitude and I just...say thank you," she said slowly.

He looked away, feeling as if he were intruding on a private moment and started again on his brushes.

She turned and laughed, walking over to help him. "I have a project today, and I was wondering if you could help me."

"I'm just finishing up now. What is it?"

"After you all rushed to the fire yesterday, I stayed to help clean up. I started talking to people like you said I should and I met some friends of friends. I realized that my good friend Taylor is a second daughter to James' girlfriend, Megan. After that, the coincidences just kept going like dominoes."

"Really? Megan?"

"Yes. Taylor was a good friend of mine in college. Seems Megan's daughter, Cassie, and Taylor have been friends their whole lives. And apparently Cassie is down here creating a breeding sanctuary for dolphins at the new resort. We all started talking, and she wants me to bring my horses up to the resort today. I guess her husband, Alex, wants to start a riding program when the resort opens fully and she was very interested in my training methods."

"So you're going to do a riding demonstration today?"

"No, I was just going to take them up to the resort and let them ride along the beach. See what it's all about. He has a corral and some new horses that need to be trained. Would you like to come?"

He took his brushes out of the liquid and dried them with the red rags he grabbed from his truck. "I think I can do that. Can Nala come?"

"Sure, she'd be fine," she said as she helped him put away his paints.

Colin threw the soaked rags in a big, empty coffee can in the back of the truck. As Hanna placed the paints in the back, she grabbed the coffee can lid and clicked it in place on top.

"No!" Colin said sharply, grabbing the can.

Hanna pulled her hand back quickly, as if stung. "I'm sorry."

"It's all right. It's just that if you put rags soaked in lacquer thinner in closed containers, they can ignite. I've seen it happen before. I'm extra careful, that's all."

She smiled as she placed the container in the truck and the lid to the side. "That's news to me, but thanks for letting me know."

"Don't laugh. We've had way too many fires lately. I certainly don't want to be responsible for another one." He laughed as he closed the door of the Jeep.

"Love those flames painted on the side," she said, motioning to the art work on the side of the Jeep.

"I might have had a wee bit too much tequila that day. James, too. Sounded like a good idea at the time."

"Nobody can miss you coming with that. I like it. It's...lively."

"Lively is one way to put it," he said, as he opened the door for Nala. He shut the door tightly behind her and said, "Okay, what do we do now? Lead the way."

CHAPTER 12

The horses entered the trailer quickly and Nala was content in the back seat of Hanna's truck as they head north to the resort. The sun sparkled off the water and the piercing blue of the sky made Colin grateful he'd brought sunglasses.

"Awfully bright here in the desert," Hanna said as she grabbed her own sunglasses. "Too bad they don't make glasses for horses," she said, her smile shining.

Colin laughed at the thought. "I think they'll be all right."

He let out a whistle as they rounded the last dune on the way to the resort. "Will you look at that?" he said, his eyes widening.

"Wow. I haven't been here at all since they started

construction." Hanna leaned her head out the window, her surprised expression equal to Colin's.

The gates to the resort right before them, they started down the winding road toward the expansive sea ahead. Gaping as they drove, they passed beautiful casitas made of the native ladrillo brick with dark wood roofs, each separated by beautifully landscaped courtyards filled with colorful succulents and trees with bright flowers of purples and reds. Smaller bushes lined the courtyards, the yellow of the Mexican bird of paradise flowers framing the ocotillo fences. Each casita had an arched door made of mahogany with sea creatures carved in them, each door unique.

"Look at that beautiful starfish," Hanna said as they slowly drove by one casita. "It's gorgeous."

"They really are doing a beautiful job of it, aren't they?" Colin peered ahead to the larger structure. "Is that the restaurant?"

"I have no idea. He said to turn right after the casitas and we'd find the corral."

She pulled to the right and gasped. The large building before them was stunning, a long, rectangular stable that looked as if it could hold at least 20 horses. Each stall was enclosed by etched wooden doors similar to those on the casitas, but these were engraved with beautiful renderings of horses. A large, fenced arena stood next to the stable, the land cleared of ocotillo and cactus to make way for riders and their mounts.

"I thought you said he was considering a riding program. Seems he's made up his mind," Colin said with a laugh as he opened the car door to let Nala out.

"We really only had a brief conversation. I had no idea it was this...far along." Hanna's red riding boots hit the dirt as she hurried toward the arena. "This is amazing."

Colin watched her eyes light up as she paced along the wooden fence of the arena. He smiled as she ran her hands along the fence lovingly and could imagine her and Violet running full bore along the side, her black hair streaming behind her. He thought it was something he would like to see.

Colin lifted his hand over his eyes as he looked out over the water. A red Jeep approached, a plume of dust from the road rising in the air.

"That must be Cassie and Alex," Hanna said as the Jeep pulled up to the stables. The tall, handsome driver stepped out of the Jeep and he waved at Hanna as he walked around to the passenger side. He opened the door, holding his hand out to a young woman who beamed at him as she took his hand. They held hands as they walked toward the arena, both with wide smiles.

The young woman hugged Hanna warmly as the man turned his smile to Colin. "Hello. I'm Alex, and this is Cassie," he said, extending his hand.

"Oh, this is my friend Colin," Hanna said, releasing Cassie from her arms. "He's the firefighter I was telling you about."

Colin shook Alex's hand and looked down. "Painter, actually. Volunteer firefighter," he said.

"And an Irishman, I see," Alex said, his smile widening.

"Ah, it's me accent, I guess."

Hanna laughed. "I know you don't think you have one, but you do."

Cassie gazed at him intently, hands on hips. "We've met, but nice to see you again. I have heard a bit more since I've been down here full time. Are you the one they say is in hiding? An ex-IRA bomber?"

Hanna gasped.

Colin tipped the brim of his hat in her direction. "That's me, ma'am. On the run from the law after I bombed the London Bridge."

"That's ridiculous. Nobody bombed the London Bridge," Cassie said, laughing.

"Well, if you believe the rumors around here, I did that and more." Colin shoved his hands in his pockets.

Alex grabbed Cassie's hand, pulling her toward the stable. "We'll forgive your sordid past." He winked at Colin. "You should hear what they say about me."

Cassie tugged her hair behind her, wrapping a hair tie around it quickly. "You'd think he was Satan himself. Many people around here can't see that the resort is a good thing. Everybody's more concerned about the nuisance. We're trying to build it with as low an impact on the environment as possible, even with the sanctuary. Protecting, not harming."

Colin and Hanna followed toward the building as Nala ran ahead. "No matter what you do, people don't like change."

"That's an understatement," Alex said, his Spanish accent more pronounced as he spoke. "We've even had some threats if you can believe it."

Cassie put her hand on his shoulder. "We're trying very hard to do the right thing by the land, and by the vaquita. It's frustrating to be met with resistance and resentment."

"Not any serious threats, I hope," Colin said, his pulse quickening with concern.

Alex's jaw tightened as he put his arm around Cassie. "I'm not giving them any of my attention. Rumors fly around here, and I'm choosing to see them as just that."

"I know all about rumors. And rumors die hard." Colin gazed out at the water as Hanna walked up behind him.

"Best we all just move forward with our plans, with confidence," Cassie said, smiling. "And we just won't mention the London Bridge." She nudged Colin into a smile.

"Your secret is safe with me," Alex chuckled as he opened up the doors to the stable. "With all the people angry with the resort, we may need somebody with your talents someday."

Colin felt the heat rise in his face as he followed the group inside.

Lunch was fascinating to Colin as Cassie and Alex explained what they had planned for the resort —and grand plans, they were. Kayaking, swimming, searching for creatures in the sea—and no golf course. It wasn't anything like what had originally planned, and Colin was impressed at the change in course that had come about with Alex and Cassie's input. He was proud of the new resort and its commitment to sustaining and conserving their way of life and knew that if everyone in the south campos could hear what he had, they'd feel the same.

Colin led Regalo and then Violet into the trailer as Hanna said her goodbyes to their hosts. Alex thanked her for bringing the horses out and explaining her training methods and Hanna beamed with pride. With a final hug from Cassie, Hanna turned and hopped in the truck. She turned the engine over and headed back toward home.

"You were awfully quiet today," she said as she pulled onto the pavement.

"Was I?" he said, shaking his head. "I didn't think so."

"You seemed far away."

"I was enjoying watching you with the horses," he said, putting on his sunglasses and turning his gaze toward the mountains.

"It was a fun day for me," she said. "I am thrilled that Alex wants to train his horses in a more humane way. I think Violet and Regalo are a good example of what can be done with that."

"You are nothing if not passionate about what you do," he said. He rubbed his hand on his knee, wiping off the dirt of the day. "I've been thinking about the fires. These two are more than we had all last year. It just seems strange to me."

"Do you have any reason to think they're more than a coincidence?"

"Nothing specific. Not really."

"But you're wondering about them?"

"A bit. Just grateful that no one's been hurt."

He fell silent again, hoping that would be the end of the conversation.

"So, there's nothing else on your mind, then?" Hanna reached over to him, placing her hand on his arm.

He turned, taking off his sunglasses and meeting her gaze. Her dark eyes seemed to see through him. His voice grew quiet as he said, "I've lived here for quite some time now, and I still feel like an outsider. I know people joke all the time about my history, but as Alex said today, some of it is a bit extreme."

"It bothers you, then?" Her voice softened, her eyes turned back to the road.

"It does, yes. I've spent a lot of time and effort with the bomberos, trying to help people. To have anyone think I could do harm goes against who I really am, what I believe in."

"Do you know how these rumors started? Is there any truth to them?"

He pulled his arm from underneath her hand, quickly putting his sunglasses back on, firmly in place. His stomach clenched as he looked away.

"Not as you'd think, but enough to bother me. I've not told anyone, and don't intend to begin now."

He felt her surprise and knew he'd hurt her. It had been a long time since he'd spoken of his past. He'd come to Mexico hoping for a clean slate and had worked hard to start his life over. The last thing he needed was for all of that to come up now.

CHAPTER 13

Colin had left Hanna's house quickly when they'd returned. Megan was there waiting for Hanna, and he decided it was a good opportunity for him to head home. With a quick greeting to Megan and a thank you to Hanna, he hopped in his Jeep and headed home.

The rash of fires and Alex's comments about his past roiled in his mind as he let Nala in the house ahead of him. The sun was setting in the way it could only over the desert, turning the clouds multiple shades of scarlet, pink and purple.

As the sky blazed, warmly lighting his kitchen, he was startled by the ring of his phone. Down here, the phone rarely rang and he wondered who would intrude on his thoughts.

Quickly answering, he heard the voice of Mike, the homeowner in Playa Luna whose house had burned the day before. Colin had called him earlier and left a message, asking for a return call.

"Hi, Mike, how are you doing?" Colin said quickly, cringing at his question to the man who had just lost his beach house.

"Very funny, Colin," the gruff voice replied.

Remembering the reason for his call, Colin said, "Sorry about that, mate. We did all we could to save the house, but the two explosions pretty much did it in."

"Two explosions? I hadn't heard about two."

"That's why I was calling. I wanted to confirm how many propane tanks you had."

"Just the one. And it was outside the house in the back."

"What did you keep in the five-gallon drum that was in the garage?"

"I didn't have one of those. I did a few years ago for oil, but got rid of them."

Colin smiled. So, he had kept his oil in them. No point talking about the danger of that now.

"But there weren't any in there now, that you knew of? I know I saw one. James and I commented on it."

"No, I didn't. Any ideas on the cause of it? I know there weren't any neighbors there, either. Fireworks, maybe?"

"I don't think fireworks started it. Everybody was at the firemen's fundraiser. Nobody in camp, as far as I can tell."

They spent a quick moment catching up, Mike making plans to come down from California as soon as possible to clean up and survey the damage.

"All those years to build that house. And gone in the blink of an eye," Mike said. "I can hardly believe it."

"So sorry, mate. Let me know when you get down and we'll round up a crew to help"

"Thanks, Colin. Good to know you were on the spot."

Colin's shoulders drooped as he ended the call and tossed the phone on the couch. He leaned on the kitchen counter, his muscles tensing at the memory of all of Mike's possessions, his beach side hopes and his dreams, buried amidst the rubble of the fire.

Nala yelped as Colin banged his fist against the counter, the frustration over his friends losing their homes more than he could bear. "Sorry, Nala," he said as he smoothed her ruffled fur. "I just need to make sense of all of this."

He reached for his phone, flipping through the ones he'd taken on it before. He enlarged them, looked at them from a different angle and still—nothing. But he knew there was something that connected the fires. He just knew it. If only he could figure out what it was.

CHAPTER 14

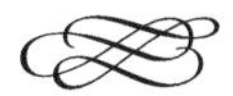

Hanna watched quietly as the dust settled on the road after Colin drove off toward home.

"What's that about, friend?" Megan said as she came up behind Hanna, resting her hand on her shoulder.

"I'm not sure. I've only recently gotten to know him, and he's a fun person to be around. Very talented, very funny.

"And handsome," Megan prodded with a smile.

Hanna looked at her friend, feeling a bit confused. "Handsome? Yes, I suppose he is," she said, her cheeks flushing. She quickly turned to the horse trailer, opening the doors to lead Violet and Regalo back to their corral.

Handing Regalo's lead to Megan, she headed toward the gate. "I guess I have noticed more how he is on the inside. And today he was different."

Megan led Regalo into the corral, unclipping his lead and giving him a pat on the flank. He ran off, running freely now he was out of the trailer.

"How so? James says he's a guy who's pretty even-keel, always up."

"That's been my experience so far, and we've had some nice talks. But today, Alex was talking about the rumors about his past, some silly things about being involved with the IRA. And I think it got to him."

"Colin and James laugh about that all the time. Everyone thinks James was a spy, too. They're just rumors, and pretty ridiculous. You think it bothered him?"

"Yes, I do. He got pretty quiet after the talk of that, and the threats the resort's been getting."

Hanna closed the gate of the corral as Megan threw hay over the fence for the horses.

"The resort's getting threats? What kind?" Megan's brows furrowed.

"He didn't really say. He doesn't seem to think they're serious."

"Well, you're the most intuitive person I know. What do you think is bothering Colin?"

"He won't tell me. I would only be guessing."

Megan laughed. "I've known you a long time, Hanna. You may call them guesses, but you're always right."

Hanna smiled at her friend. She turned toward the setting sun, the colors magnificent against the darkening sky. "All the stories about his past may be just rumors, but there's something there that rings true for him. That causes him pain."

Megan sat down on the bench beside her friend, admiring the sunset as well. "You don't actually think he was involved in any of that stuff, do you?"

"I don't know for sure. I would like to think not. But he won't talk to me. As much as I like him, I don't know where to go with that. And my sense is that while he may have not been truly involved in anything illegal, somehow there's more."

"I hate to say it, but if you're going to leave a different kind of life behind and start over, Mexico's a pretty good place to do it. Re-invent yourself, create a new start. But he's so committed to helping people here in the South Campos. That just doesn't make any sense, that he'd be running from something."

The sun made its final appearance of the day, finally setting behind the mountain in a blaze of color. Hanna sighed as she turned to her friend. "I would love that to be the case. I guess we'll just have to wait and see."

Her friend stood up, pulling Hanna up with her and heading toward the house.

"Just give it some time, maybe. You've only just met and there's no hurry to find out anything at all."

Hanna walked slowly toward the house, her eyes cast downward, her red boots shuffling in the dirt.

"What? You really like him, don't you?" Megan said, swinging her arm over Hanna's shoulder.

Hanna blushed and shoved her hands in her pockets. "I don't have time for anything like that. I've got horses to train."

Megan snickered. "Ah, I get it. Gotta stay serious and committed. Make sure you don't have any fun. Make sure nothing happens that isn't planned."

"That's not fair, Megan. I'm not that...rigid." She crossed her arms over her chest.

"Ordinarily, no. I haven't seen this side of you in ages. You've been pretty Zen for a long time. It figures, that's when you'd be thrown for a loop."

Hanna started walking faster. "I have not been

thrown for a loop. I just think he's a nice guy, that's all."

"Uh-huh. That's why you're bothered that he won't tell you his deepest, darkest secrets."

Hanna smiled. "I don't want to know his deepest darkest secrets. Just trying to help a friend."

Megan held her hand up to her mouth in mock surprise.

"Okay. I'll go with that, for now. I bet you'll find out everything you want to know, and soon. I saw how he looked at you."

Hanna's head snapped in her direction, her pony-tail flipping over her shoulder, her brown eyes wide. "What do you mean?"

Megan's blue eyes flashed at her friend's surprise. "Come on. You can't tell me you haven't noticed that silly grin on his face when you're around."

The groan Hanna let out made Megan laugh even harder. "You're making that up. We're just friends."

"As I said, for now. Who could resist a beautiful girl in red cowboy boots, anyway?" She grabbed Hanna's hand and pulled her toward the house. "Come on. I brought a bottle of wine and it's way past happy hour.

CHAPTER 15

Colin's mood was still dark when he fell into bed. His night was restless, and he'd tossed and turned for hours. Memories of his childhood had come unbidden, and thoughts of his youth in Ireland were front and center. He had gotten up to pace several times, the millions of stars shining like sparks on black velvet not able to calm him back to sleep.

With eyes wide open, he watched the Milky Way pass overhead and the sky lighten over the Sea of Cortez, equally as glorious as the sunset the previous evening. Even Nala wasn't awake this early and he was spared the slobbery tennis ball on his head. Chuckling over his good fortune, he decided to give up on sleep and take a run on the beach.

He pulled a t-shirt over his lean, muscled frame and yanked on a pair of shorts. He smoothed his wavy hair quickly with the palm of his hand and pulled a baseball cap on. Quickly pulling on his running shoes, he hollered for Nala to follow and headed up the beach.

Lost in his thoughts again, he enjoyed the release as sweat began to glisten on his skin. Running faster, he felt his breathing quicken and his heart pound, as it had when he ran in the hills of Ireland as a boy. Before he knew it, he was a few miles up the beach in front of the garage that had burned several nights before. He bent over, resting his hands on his knees for several moments as he caught his breath.

"Hey, Colin," he heard a voice call. Holding his hand over his brow, he spotted the homeowner waving him over. He walked toward the house, the smell of coffee wafting on the breeze, reminding him he hadn't yet had his daily dose.

"Coffee?" the man said, lifting up a mug.

Colin smiled. "Sure. Thanks."

"You're welcome. Anything I can do for a bombero."

Colin smiled and took the mug that was offered him, pouring in some cream. "I've been thinking about your fire the other night. I'm still trying to make sense of it, especially after the one we had the next day."

"Do you think there was anything unusual about it?"

"Honestly, I'm not sure. I'm not a professional at this. Just trying to check into everything I can think of for an explanation. If it was fireworks, maybe we need to do some kind of education for weekenders so this doesn't happen."

"That would be comforting. Besides all of the dogs hiding under the beds, it's a bit scary when they set off so many," he said, shaking his head slowly.

"Could there have been anything in the garage that may have ignited? Did you have any big five-gallon drums in there? I took pictures but haven't looked at them yet."

"No, nothing like that. As I told you that night, we got all of the flammable stuff out before the roof collapsed. Haven't been back in to do anything with it yet, though."

"Mind if I take a quick look?" Colin set his mug down, hoping he might see something new if he rummaged through the garage again.

"Not at all. Go ahead. I've been too depressed to go in there. Guess I should join you."

The two men headed over to the charred garage,

the blackened brick walls half standing. They climbed over the things that had been saved from the fire: kayaks, beach chairs, umbrellas and ice chests.

"Guess we got quite a few things out before it really went up," the man said, stepping gingerly over a deflated beach volleyball.

Colin walked through the rubble again, picking up a piece of metal and rummaging here and there. Moving away some debris in the corner, he spotted a small can of lacquer thinner with the lid off. His eyes narrowed as memories came flooding back to him.

"Are you a painter by chance?" he said over his shoulder.

The man appeared startled. "No. Why do you ask?"

"Is this your can of lacquer thinner? Here, in the corner."

"I've never seen that before. Like I told you, there was nothing flammable in here, no supplies of any kind like that. Just the gas, and we got that out."

Colin crossed his arms over his chest, one hand stroking his chin. This looked like a familiar scene to him, one from a long time ago.

"And you said you heard fireworks that night and thought that had caused the blaze. No explosion?"

"If it was an explosion, it was certainly a small one. Not much louder than a firecracker."

They talked a little bit longer about what might have happened, but they ran into a dead end. Colin's head spun as he jogged home, the scene of the fire flashing in his mind. It hadn't even occurred to him that this might be the work of an arsonist, but now the possibility was becoming real.

As he ran, his memories overtook him. He vividly recalled the fires his father responded to as a volunteer firefighter with Colin tagging along...until it got too dangerous. He'd been about sixteen when things got really dicey. Boys he'd been friends with his entire life were experimenting with ways to start fires, bragging loudly about wanting to be a part of "the cause". It wasn't long before it got out of hand and people began to get hurt.

Before that last night that had changed his life forever, his father would come home and explain how they did it. He showed Colin the cans of lacquer thinner with rags for small fires. He explained how they used larger drums full of flammables with makeshift fuses and timers.

It suddenly felt too familiar and Colin raced home, wanting to see if he could spot anything in the pictures he'd taken that might confirm what he was beginning to suspect.

He replayed the sights of the second fire in his mind, the houses rushing past in a blur. Nala was at his heel and he barely noticed which part of the beach he was on, trying to remember what he saw surrounding the small can at the first house and the 5-gallon drum at Mike's house. As he slowed to catch his breath, he turned inland. Looking up at the campos, his breath caught in his throat.

A pillar of smoke climbed high in the sky from one of the campos. It got bigger as he neared and the smoke was as black as he'd ever seen smoke be. It wasn't that far in the distance...it was clear that it was in one of the campos. He cursed himself for leaving without his radio. If he'd had it with him, he might be lucky enough to hear that it was nothing. But, instead, his heart raced and he was drenched in sweat, and not because of the run.

As he ran faster, he hoped that his eyes were playing tricks on him.

Maybe it's just somebody burning trash. Please, be that.

His eyes glued to the plume of smoke, he ran faster toward it, hoping against hope that it was nothing out of the ordinary.

Nala bounded ahead as he ran up through the arroyo. As he reached the top of the ridge, he couldn't deny it any longer. He could now see flames as well as smoke and his heart pounded. Although there were several houses in between him and the flames, there was no doubt that it was Hanna's house.

CHAPTER 16

Blood pumped quickly through his veins and his heart pounded as he started off toward the fire, jumping over stumps and weaving through the cactus. As he rounded the last house before Hanna's, his breath caught in his throat and he stopped dead in his tracks.

In the corral to the side of the house, Hanna held the reins of both Regalo and Violet, leading them calmly over to the far side of the corral. Neither horse seemed alarmed, and confusion washed over Colin's face.

"Hanna!" he yelled as he continued running toward the smoke. It didn't appear to be coming from her house, but from the garage on the side.

"Colin," she said as she finished tying the horses

as far as possible from the smoke, "I haven't been able to do anything about the fire yet." She turned toward the garage. "I just noticed the smoke and wanted to get them out of the way first. I called for the bomberos." She calmly walked toward the burning structure, her red cowboy boots raising dust in her wake.

"Stay away, Hanna," he said.

Her eyes flashed as she turned to him, stopping mid-stride. "This is my house, and I intend to do what I need to do."

They both turned in unison toward the road as they heard the sirens of the fire engines. The lights flashed as they turned toward the house, heading down the dirt road at a pace Colin was familiar with, trying to navigate the ruts and washes. This time, his hands clenched in frustration as he wished they could respond more quickly, get to this fire faster.

Hanna turned back toward the garage, striding forward toward the hoses that were used to fill the horses' water tanks. He caught up with her just as she was turning the spigot. Grabbing her hand, he pulled her back toward the far side of the corral. "I think we should wait for the fire trucks, Hanna. I have a bad feeling about this."

She stood and looked at him, her eyes quizzical

and confused. They both turned toward the garage as flames peeked through the top of the roof, licking at the smoke.

"Trust me, Hanna," he said, his jaw clenching as he held out his hand to her.

He watched as the black plumes rose higher now, and as he turned to her, her face changed. Her eyes never left his, and as she reached out her hand, her fingers inches from his, the explosion sent them both hurtling away from the fire, flying through the air and landing on the other side of the corral at the feet of Violet and Regalo.

CHAPTER 17

Hanna's eyes flickered as she slowly regained consciousness. She looked up at the blue sky and remembered she was in Mexico. Violet was nuzzling her cheek as she lay on the ground, as if prodding her awake.

She groaned and patted Violet's head, pushing her head away. "I'm all right, girl," she said as she tried to sit up. She made it to her elbow before she saw Colin next to her, sprawled on the ground and unconscious.

In a flash, she recalled what had happened. She remembered deciding to trust him, ready to run, and the sound of the blast that sent them flying. Now, the fire was much bigger and had either jumped or been sent over to the house several yards away.

Although her house was made of the local ladrillo, she knew there was much to burn.

As she turned back to Colin, she saw the first fire engine pull up to the scene. She laid her hand softly on his cheek and called his name as the bomberos prepared to battle the fire, James rushing to where they had been thrown.

"Hanna, are you all right? What happened?" James said quickly, his eyes full of concern.

"Oh, man," Colin said, his eyes opening as Hanna wiped the soot from his face. "Let me help," he said as he slowly came to, his voice groggy and uneven.

"No, not a chance," Hanna said as she helped him to a sitting position.

"We called an ambulance from San Felipe, but you know it'll take a while to get here. Just sit tight and let us get this out as quickly as we can."

As James left to help the other bomberos, the captain pulled up.

"Why are you here out of uniform, son?" the captain said as he walked over to Colin. His smile faded as he looked from Colin to Hanna and back again, soot covering both of their faces and their clothes blackened.

"Sorry, Captain. I was out for a run and saw the

smoke on the way back. I'd forgotten to take my radio," he said, shaking his head.

"Don't be so hard on yourself, Colin," the captain said, turning back to the blaze. "Let's see what we can do about this one. You stay here and catch your breath. Ambulance is on its way."

It was all she could do to keep Colin away from the fire and sitting calmly as they waited for the ambulance to arrive. The tortured look on his face as he watched his friends battle the blaze in front of them tugged at her heart.

"Colin, there's nothing you can do now," she said, reaching for his hand. "They're doing all they can, and it has to take its course."

"That's what's killing me," he said. "The one fire I should be fighting hardest, and I can't do a thing."

Suddenly, all of the bomberos backed away from the fire, heading to the fire trucks, their water from their hoses turning into a dribble.

"What's happening?" she asked, wondering what would make them stop fighting the flames now, as they reached higher toward the sky.

"Oh, no," Colin groaned, his head sinking into his hands. "They've run out of water. Only one of our trucks works. They'll have to go back to the station for more."

The bomberos packed up the water hoses as they prepared to drive back to the station for more water. As the captain coordinated the men, he turned to them and said, "Colin, you head with Javier back to the station to fill it up. The rest of us will stay here and see if we can get some hoses on it, or buckets at least."

"I'd really like to stay, Captain. Can you send someone else back?" Colin said, his eyes wide as he watched the fire.

"No, son, you're low man on the totem pole. You need to go back and fill up the engine," the captain said over his shoulder as he and the other men left to see what hoses were available.

Colin's fists clenched as he turned away from the fire. Hanna watched as he slowly walked to the truck, kicking the tire before he climbed into the passenger seat.

As the ambulance drove up and the EMT's checked over their vital signs, Hanna couldn't help but notice Colin, his eyes not leaving the blaze for one moment. He mechanically held out his arms when they asked him to, and tried to cooperate, but she watched as he mentally experienced every move with James and the other bomberos. She thought maybe he'd jump out of the truck and go, so she stayed as close by as she could.

The relief on his face when the truck had returned, once again full of water, melted her heart. His concern was very moving, and she sensed that the torture of not being able to help was almost more than he could bear.

She glanced at her home in flames, thinking of all of her stained glass melting and pictures of her family turning to ashes. Shaking the thought from her head, she turned to Colin."

"It's just stuff, Colin. Things. Things that can be replaced. The important thing to me is that Violet, Regalo, you and I are all fine. And Nala, too," she said as Nala appeared to lick Colin's face. Shakily, he lifted a hand to pet her, his eyes still not leaving the blaze.

As the time passed and they were checked by the EMT's, the blaze slowed to a crawl and the bomberos got the upper hand. By the time the flames had subsided, most of the house was gone and the rest had been filled with smoke.

"I'm so sorry, ma'am. We did as much as we could with our limited resources." The captain held his helmet in his hand as he approached Hanna and Colin. His eyes were filled with sadness and Hanna felt he truly was devastated. "These fires are so incredibly frustrating. They move faster than anything I've ever seen around here, and start off with a bang." He turned to glance at the smoldering embers, turning over the yellow helmet in his hands.

Hanna stood and walked toward the captain, her knees still a bit wobbly. "I know you did everything you could, Captain. I've very grateful you're here at all."

The captain nodded at her with a look of regret on his face, accepting the gratitude.

"I know he feels as awful as I do," Colin said as the crew climbed into the truck and drove away. "I'm sure you'll have a cleanup crew here first thing in the morning, if I know the captain."

She smiled. "It's nice to have such good friends around here. But there's no way I can stay here tonight," she said as she looked at the blackened remains of her house.

"Well, you'll just have to stay with me, then." Colin stood, taking a moment to get his legs solidly underneath him as well.

She looked at him, this tall Irishman she'd gotten to know, and wondered why she trusted him so completely. It was not her way to be trusting of people unless shown a reason to feel otherwise. But something about this man, with his green eyes and unruly hair, made her feel safe.

She laughed out loud at that thought, as her house had just burned to the ground. But she knew she trusted him, fire aside. It wasn't like he'd had anything to do with it; he'd only tried to help. She was grateful she'd followed her instinct when he asked her to leave the fire. He'd saved her life.

"Thank you for the invitation. I believe I'll take you up on it."

CHAPTER 18

"This is a little bit awkward." Colin opened the front door, letting Hanna enter his house in front of him. Nala brought up the rear, bounding into the kitchen and standing by her food bowl.

Hanna walked into the kitchen, picking up Nala's empty water bowl and filling it. "Why? I can stay somewhere else if you'd like." She smiled and said, "You have secrets in here you don't want anybody to know about?"

"Why does everybody keep saying that?" he said, throwing his hat on the table. He shoved the chairs in roughly around the table and began to straighten the dishes he'd left on the counter, shoving them roughly into the sink.

"Careful, you'll break one." Hanna gently took the plates from him and set them down on the counter. "I was teasing. I'm sorry if I struck a nerve." She took his hand and turned him toward her.

"I have no secrets here or anywhere, Hanna. Just a messy house, occupied by a bachelor and his dog." He turned away as Nala pawed at her empty food bowl. Filling it and setting it on the floor, he opened the refrigerator and poured two Tecates into glasses, handing her one. "I think we both may need a beer."

She pulled out a bar stool for him, patting the cushion for him to sit. "How about I make us something to eat," she said, picking up an avocado from a bowl full of them on the counter. "Anyone for guacamole?"

Colin laughed. "My favorite, and those are just about to be too soft to use."

She rummaged through his kitchen for the needed supplies—onions, jalapenos, salt, pepper, garlic and hot sauce. As she chopped, she said, "You seem a little sensitive about the rumors. Do they bother you?"

Colin took a big sip from his mug, the beer washing the soot from his throat. "I know people talk. I just wish they'd talk about someone else. I guess I can't blame them. I'm pretty far from home."

"But you're concerned about something," she stated matter-of-factly.

"I am. You seem pretty calm about what just happened."

Hanna stopped chopping for a moment. "I am very disappointed. Make no mistake about that. But Violet and Regalo are safe. I can make more stained glass, although it was painful to watch them melt."

"You're amazing," Colin said. He watched her pick up the knife again and continue to chop. She was so peaceful, so calm. At the moment, he didn't share her peacefulness.

"But you lost your home. We could have lost our lives. I'm not so sure it was an accident," Colin said, setting his mug back on the counter with a thud. "I haven't wanted to say anything yet as I'm not positive. But I don't think these fires are all coincidences."

Her knife stopped in mid-air as she quickly turned to look at him. "You're serious, aren't you?"

His shoulders hunched as he absently flipped the bottle caps in his hand. "I've been back to both of the fire scenes before this one. In each instance, there were objects in the buildings that the owners were unaware of. Objects that shouldn't have been there, and contained flammable liquids."

She stared at him for a moment, her mouth open in surprise. "How do you know that? That they were things that could have started a fire?"

He looked up, meeting her gaze. He was silent for a moment as he wrestled with the decision that he had tried not to make, thought of the past he had tried to forget.

She set the knife down on the counter and walked around to the side he was sitting on. He turned toward her, his eyes downcast. Gently, she lifted his chin, turning his face toward hers.

He looked up into her dark, soulful eyes. He felt the weight of his story, the ache of missing his family and as it all rushed back in his mind, he felt his heart quicken.

He'd been mystified and enamored with this woman since he'd met her and now, that feeling intensified. He stood and brushed her cheek, leaning in and meeting her gaze.

She stood on her tiptoes, and his heart soared as her warm lips met his, lending comfort that he should have been giving to her. Her house had been lost, and here she was comforting and encouraging him. He closed his eyes, basking in the feel of her comforting touch.

She took a step back, her eyes not leaving his. She

held out her hand, inviting him into her heart. "Trust me," she said.

And he knew in that moment that he did trust her.

It all came rushing out as if a dam had broken inside of him. He shared his love of Ireland, his close ties with his family and the pain in his heart that he could no longer see them. He spoke with joy of riding with his father as a volunteer firefighter and how proud he'd been to help his neighbors at his father's side.

His voice slowed as he described the devices his father brought home, showing him the damage and teaching him what to look for. His voice broke as he shared his father's decision that he could no longer accompany him as the boys in the neighborhood had started to set fires for fun, hoping to be called to "the cause". His eyes shone with pride as he described his father's passion for respecting all people, of all backgrounds, and his refusal to take sides in a cause that was ripping their community apart.

He stopped to take a breath and looked over at Hanna. She'd been silent throughout his rambling, giving him the space to speak, to feel, quietly finishing the guacamole and getting him another beer as needed.

"That's quite a story, Colin. You must miss your family very much."

"Aye, I do. Every day, I think of them. Every day, I wonder how they are." His eyes fell again, and she reached for his hand.

He took it, the warmth it spread within him a surprise. Holding her hand, he felt like he could continue, like he wanted to continue. Finally.

"After the thugs who used to be my friends got a foothold in the community and everyone was frightened, they looked about for more recruits. I had experience with fires and knowledge that they wanted." He stopped, searching for the words to explain what happened next.

"Go on," she said gently, her hand not leaving his, her eyes gentle.

"They came to the house and threatened my father. Said they'd kill him if I didn't take up with them and help. By then, it had nothing to do with any cause. They were just hooligans, thugs, threatening storekeepers and homeowners with arson if they didn't pay for protection."

Hanna drew in a sharp breath. "How awful," she said as she rested her hand on his knee.

"I remember looking at my mother and my sister.

They were terrified for us all. I couldn't bear it. I couldn't put my father at risk."

Colin's face fell into his hands as the memories grew and grew. He hadn't wanted to remember. He hadn't wanted to talk about it. Hanna's eyes welled up as he continued.

"I didn't know what to do. I watched my mother and sister cry. I heard my father say it didn't matter, there was nothing they could do. 'Stand strong,' he told me. As I went to bed that night, I watched out my bedroom window as an explosion ripped through the local school. The lads ran by in front of the house, yelling and cursing at my father. And calling my name."

Hanna sat back against the couch, the tears now spilling down her cheeks. Her voice was soft, and she spoke so quietly he barely heard her. "What did you do?"

"I grabbed everything I had, which wasn't much. Shoved it in a knapsack and ran downstairs. My mother was standing in the kitchen, crying. She looked up at me and held out a small purse. It was all the money she had. She hugged me, and I left."

"Oh," she said, her breath rushing out of her, her face buried in her hands. "How could you bear it?"

"I had no choice, Hanna. If I'd stayed, I'd have had

to become one of them or risked my father's life. It was the only thing I could think of to save my family."

"Are they all right?"

"Yes. The thugs were after them for a bit, but they gave up after they realized I had gone for good. I've only heard through relatives. But I know they're all right."

"I'm shocked that these kinds of things happen. I don't even know what to say."

"Well, that's the problem, love. I do know that these things happen, and I'm afraid it's happening right here. In our hometown."

CHAPTER 19

The guacamole didn't last long after Hanna finished making it. Grabbing two more beers and a bowl of chips, she'd carried it all out onto the patio, hoping some fresh air would do them good. A shower was very appealing, but she decided she could wait. They were both still sooty from the day's events, but Colin's outburst had come as a bit of a surprise, and she wasn't ready to part with him quite yet. Colin's description of leaving his home, his family, had left her exhausted, both of them, it seemed, and they found themselves falling silent.

As the sun set behind them over the mountains, they watched the sky turn pink, then purple, as the light disappeared and the moon rose over the horizon. The waves lapped gently on the shore, the tide in close.

The peaceful moment, by the light of the moon, seemed to bring him around with a renewed energy. She watched as he slowly came back into the present, leaving the past behind for now.

He took a chip from the bowl and scraped the last of the guacamole from the bowl. He rubbed his hand over his still-sooty face. "I'm sorry about all of that, Hanna. Seems once I started, I couldn't stop."

"I'm not sorry at all," she said. "I knew there was something you were keeping from me. I'm honored that you chose to tell me."

"I don't think I had a choice, now, did I?" He rubbed his hand on the back of his neck, seeming surprised that it was black from soot.

Startled, she stood and took the empty bowls in the house. "What do you mean, you didn't have a choice?"

He came up behind her and she closed her eyes as he wrapped his hands around her waist, his chest against her back. "You told me to trust you. And I do. I was surprised to find that out."

Her breath quickened as she felt his warmth around her. "I'm so glad you decided to trust me. As I trusted you earlier."

Her eyes flew opened as he laughed in her ear. "I think we probably should wash up." He held up his hand with black soot on it and ran a quick finger down her cheek. "You're a little dirty. I probably look the same." He pulled her over in front of the mirror in the hallways and they both burst into laughter.

"Why didn't you tell me I look like a raccoon?" she said.

"We both washed our hands, at least. And I think you look beautiful."

Butterflies fluttered in her stomach as she turned back toward the kitchen. "I don't have any clothes. I think I'll take a shower and borrow some of yours if that's all right. I can ask Megan for a loan tomorrow."

"Sure, no problem at all. Follow me," he said as he led her toward the guest room and bathroom. On the way, he grabbed some clothes and clean towels. "Let me know if you need anything. I'll be in the other room getting cleaned up, too."

"Thank you," she said as she shut the door. She undressed quickly, sorry only that her red cowboy boots were ruined, and put her clothes in the trash can. Standing under the shower, she turned it on as hot as she could stand, washing away the events of the day.

She thought of the fire, of her horses, of Colin's confession. Everything was a jumble in her mind, and she wasn't sure what he had meant about the danger of the fires. Did he believe they had been set on purpose? By an arsonist? She just couldn't imagine anyone doing that.

She decided to ask him more about it later, and for now to just let the steaming water wash it all away.

HANNA WAS STILL in the shower when Colin came out into the living room, the soot removed and wearing a clean t-shirt and jeans. He stood on the patio near the ocean and looked up at the stars, wondering what had made him tell Hanna about his family. It was something he hadn't felt before, like a need for her to know him better, to understand. Whatever it had been, it was done now. No taking it back.

He gathered an armful of kindling and logs from the stack on the side of the house. A bit of a chill was in the air and he decided to light a fire in the big kiva in the side of his living room. When he had built the house, he'd hired the best fireplace builder in the South Campos. He was very specific about what he wanted, and Wes, the builder, had done his best work ever.

The kiva stood from floor to ceiling, built into the corner, a tiled seat all the way around it. It reminded him of the fireplaces in the adobe houses in New Mexico, and he spent many nights reading by the light it produced, basking in its warmth. Now, he wanted to share that with Hanna.

She walked into the room, her long, black hair shiny and wet, hugging his flannel shirt around her and looking a little lost in the sweats he'd given her that were way too big. Her eyes grew wide at the fire and she walked quickly over to it, sitting along its edge.

"This is a beautiful kiva," she said, holding out her hands to warm them.

He held out his hands closer to the fire next to hers. "Thank you. I love it, too. It reminds me of home."

She quickly pulled her hands back and looked at him. He held out a glass of wine to her. "Thought you might appreciate this."

"Yes, thank you." Her eyes sparkled by the light of the flames. "So, now that we don't look like chimney sweeps any longer, tell me what you're thinking about the fires now."

As he finished explaining about each fire having what he would consider to be an explosive device, and believing that those explosive devices ignited the fires, Hanna fell silent for a moment.

When she finally spoke, she said, "So, you believe that the lacquer thinner can in the first fire had been full of something and had been ignited, starting the fire?"

"Yes, exactly. I saw the can the second time I was there, hidden under some rubble. The homeowner said he did hear pops, like an explosion, but assumed that it was fireworks on the beach."

"And on the second fire, we all know there were two explosions. Everybody heard them."

"Yes, but Mike swears that he had only one propane tank and there was nothing else in the structure that could have, or would have exploded." Colin was pacing now as Hanna asked more questions.

"Today, at my house, we both know there as an explosion," she said, smiling slightly.

Colin rubbed the bump on his head slowly. "Yes, that's a pretty safe statement," he said.

"Well, I can tell you that there was nothing in

there that could have exploded. It was just a secondary garage that I kept tack in...horse feed and saddles. Nothing at all that could have gone up like that."

"That's not your primary garage? No gas? Nothing flammable? Not even any cleaners?"

"No, I am positive."

"Did you see anyone in it or around it? Someone who didn't belong?"

"I hadn't been in there yet this morning, but I had been out walking the horses around the corral. I was just getting ready to go in and get their saddles when I saw the smoke."

"When was the last time you were in there?"

"When we came home from the resort last night, Megan and I fed the horses and put the saddles away. There wasn't anything in there out of the ordinary." She filled his wineglass, handing it to him as he continued to pace.

"So, if someone had placed something in there, an explosive, it would have had to be last night or early this morning.

"Yes, I guess so," she said, adding another log to the fire. "But how would it have ignited? Certainly someone's not gone as far as to have something that sophisticated. Here, in Baja? I just can't believe it."

"I don't want to believe it either, Hanna, but something's not right. First thing in the morning, we can head over to your house and see what's left in the rubble. Maybe we'll find something that can point us in the right direction."

Suddenly, Colin stopped pacing. He slapped his forehead with his palm, almost spilling his wine. He set it down quickly and rushed into the kitchen.

"What's up? Where are you going?" Hanna asked as he ran back in with his camera.

"With all the commotion, I forgot I'd taken pictures of the fire scene. I want to take a closer look at the pictures of the things I think may have caused the explosions. Maybe we can see something that I missed the first time. I wasn't looking for an arsonist then. Maybe I'll see something new now.

CHAPTER 20

"There has to be something in these that I've missed," Colin said, flipping through the pictures on his phone. "Here are the pictures of the first fire."

Hanna slid her thumbs over the screen of the phone, enlarging picture after picture. "I don't see anything out of the ordinary. You said you saw a can of lacquer thinner in there afterward?" She handed over the phone. "Find the picture that shows that area."

Silent, he flipped through the pictures one by one, his frustration clear on his face. "I'm not sure I took one," he said, looking at picture after picture. "Ah, here it is. Right here, in this corner. Under this pile of debris."

Hanna turned on his computer, plugging in the phone to transfer it to the bigger screen. As they waited for it to boot up, Colin started a pot of coffee, pacing as the aroma filled the room. He didn't want to believe that somebody could be doing this on purpose, but the signs were adding up.

"Colin, look at this," Hanna said, staring at the screen. "I don't know if it means anything or not."

He rested his hands on the back of her chair, leaning over her shoulder and peering at the screen. "Can you make it bigger?" he said, his stomach dropping as he noticed something familiar.

"What is that?" she asked, pointing to the screen near where he'd said he'd found the can.

He stood up, stepping back from her chair. Rubbing his eyes with his hands, he shook his head, not wanting to believe what he saw on the screen.

"What is it?" she asked again, reaching for his hand.

He walked toward the window, his gaze steady on the ocean. "They're wires, Hanna. Wires and a timer."

Her gasp startled him and he turned to her. His heart ached at the fear in her eyes.

"But they weren't there when you went back the next day. And the can was covered up."

"Right. Means somebody went back and took them before they could be found. Wanted it to look like an accident. We might have found the same thing if we'd gone back to Mike's earlier. Too late now."

"Well, it's only been a couple of hours since the fire at my house. Think anything might be there?"

"Oh, no. People who do this kind of thing are dangerous. I'm not having you involved. Don't even think about it." His hands on her shoulders, he pushed her back down on her chair."

Brushing his hands away, she stood up, her hands on her hips. "If you think you're going by yourself, you don't know me at all, Colin." Her expression had changed from fear to anger in a flash. "It was my house, after all, and if someone's doing this on purpose, I want to find out." She pulled on her sooty boots and grabbed her hair into a ponytail, throwing on a baseball cap from the rack by the door. "If you think for one minute—"

He raised his hands in surrender. "Okay, okay. We'll see what we can find, but he may have already been there to remove the evidence."

"Well, we'll never know unless we go check. And the sooner the better," she said, grabbing her coat.

He'd grabbed a couple flashlights before he'd

headed out the door. Nala refused to stay behind, tossing her ball at him before he'd gotten out the door. "Not now, girl," he said as he closed the door behind the three of them. "Later. I promise."

As they drove to Hanna's house, she grew silent, her eyes trained out the window toward the desert. "It's so beautiful here," she said as the moon glowed, casting night shadows of the giant saguaro and ocotillos. "It's just so hard to believe that someone would be so disrespectful."

"Disrespectful?" Colin said, glancing in her direction as they turned down the dirt road to her campo.

"Yes, disrespectful. To people, to nature, to the community," she said, her eyes brimming with tears.

"I suppose that's one way to look at it. I couldn't begin to guess why people do these things. I just wish they would stop."

She wiped the tears that had spilled down her cheeks with her sleeve. "I guess I just believe in the good in people. And I'm always surprised when it's not to be found."

"Cheer up, lass," he said. His jaw clenched as they approached her house, the moon lighting up the rubble. "We could still be wrong about this." He hoped he'd sounded convincing. "I'd much rather it be nothing rather than something," he said, attempting a smile.

They pulled up to the house, Colin pulling around the back, away from the road. As they walked around to the corral, Violet and Regalo greeted them loudly. Nala jumped out of the Jeep and slipped through the posts of the corral, heading toward the horses.

"Nala, stay away," Colin called as he whistled for her. Handing Hanna a flashlight, he headed toward the building which hours before had been engulfed in flames.

"You said it started in here, right?" he said, motioning to the horse shed.

She came up behind him, her flashlight pointing to where she believed the fire had begun.

He handed her the hard hat he'd grabbed from the car and placed his own firmly on his head. "Here, put this on."

She took off her baseball cap, shoving it in the waistband of her oversized sweats. Putting the hard hat on, she said, "This has to be the most ridiculous outfit I've ever worn."

"I promise I won't take your picture," he said with a smile as he moved forward into the remains of the shed.

Grabbing her hand, he pulled her behind him slowly as he moved debris aside. "You're sure there were no propane tanks in here?"

"No, none. Like I said, only horse feed, tack and water." She gingerly poked at the charred saddles and bridles as they crumbled at her touch.

They stood in the building, moving their flashlights around slowly, illuminating every corner in turn. On the last corner, they both stopped. From behind a rack of bridles still hanging on the wall, Colin noticed something different.

"What's that?" she said, her flashlight trained in the same area.

Colin moved toward the rack, his hand reaching out to one of the strings hanging with the other bridles. "It doesn't look like leather."

As he held it in his hand, he followed it up beyond the rack, tugging gently. It led up the brick wall, ending at a ledge about a foot over his head.

Hanna moved her flashlight upward, following the wire. She gasped with surprise as it the light rested on the shelf just above their heads. "That wasn't there yesterday. I didn't have any shelves in here.

"I need something to stand on. I can't see over the

ledge." Colin looked around for something intact to give him a boost.

Hanna turned her flashlight outside, spotting a five-gallon bucket that had held water in the shed and had been thrown outside in the blast.

"Perfect," he said as she handed him the bucket. He turned it over, stepping on it to get a better view of what was on the shelf. "Oh, no."

"What? You have to stop doing that. Just say it. You're killing me."

He handed down a gallon can, empty, and several wires. She looked at them as he climbed down from the bucket. "What is this?"

"Smell it," he said as he inspected the wires he held in his hand.

She took a whiff of the can, her nose crinkling. "Ugh. Lacquer thinner. So glad you showed me what it smelled like before," she said, her eyes narrowing. "I didn't have anything like this in here. I'm positive."

"And I'm betting you didn't have one of these, either." He held out his hand, showing her the timer.

Her eyes widened as she saw what was in his hand. "A timer. A can of lacquer thinner. Not an accident," he said slowly as he grasped the meaning of what they'd found.

"I don't like this at all," she said, drawing her

jacket closer around her. "If the pictures you took of the other fires were accurate, he'd come back later and remove the evidence, at least the wires and timers," she said, shivering.

"Right. He hasn't had time to come back to this one. We'd better get out of here," he said. Whistling for Nala, he grabbed Hanna's hand, quickly pulling her toward the Jeep.

CHAPTER 21

The full Baja moon was dead overhead, shining so brightly that they turned their flashlights off as they walked quickly to the car. They started to round the remains of the building, heading to where Colin had parked in the back of the house, and stopped dead in their tracks as the headlights of a car approached.

"Who'd be out here so late at night?" Hanna asked, holding Colin's hand tightly.

"Not like anyone should be on this road," he said, pulling her quickly behind the only remaining patio wall.

As the car came closer, it slowed, the driver turning off the headlights. It crept slowly forward, eventually pulling alongside the arena. It stopped, the engine idling, as Colin and Hanna watched.

"Do you think that's the arsonist?" Hanna whispered. "I don't know who else would be out here."

"Could be anybody in a Jeep like that. Everybody has them," he said, taking note of the dark blue Jeep, just like his. They were almost standard issue here in Baja and many people had them.

"Well, it's my house. I'm going to see who it is," Hanna said, stepping out from behind the wall before Colin could stop her.

The car door had opened before she started over, the driver with one foot on the ground. Hanna turned on her flashlight, shining it in the direction of the car. Colin turned on his flashlight with a sigh and headed out after her.

They'd taken only a few steps, their lights trained on the car, when the driver slammed the door, gunning the engine and doing a u-turn. Rocks flew in the air as the car sped back toward the main road, dust shooting behind it, Nala chasing behind.

Colin whistled for Nala, and she gave up the chase, running quickly back to him and sitting by his side.

They both stared at the retreating car, their flashlights hanging limply at their sides.

"Did you see that?" Hanna finally said, her voice low.

"Uh, yeah," he said, not believing his eyes.

"I get that it was a blue Jeep. There are tons of them around here."

"Right," Colin said. "But I thought I had the only one with flames painted on the sides. That one was exactly like mine."

CHAPTER 22

Colin woke slowly, his head fuzzy, and it took a few moments for him to realize he had fallen asleep on his couch. Hanna was beside him, and he pulled a blanket over her as he got up, tucking it under her chin. Her black hair was tousled, part of it falling over her eyes. He smoothed it back gently, surprised at the feelings he had for this woman he'd only recently met.

We have been through a lot together in a very short time. He watched her sleep and knew he wanted to keep her safe, out of danger. *Am I the one who's put her in danger in the first place?* He shook off the thought and headed to the kitchen to start the coffee.

They'd traveled back to Colin's house almost in a daze. "Too much information," he'd said as he put another log in the kiva. They'd talked about the fires, the Jeep, the timers, trying to make sense of it all.

She'd insisted that they find out who was behind it. She wanted to make it right, to stop the fires. But how? All they had was some pictures, some wires, some timers and some ideas. By the time they'd talked it over, she'd convinced him to get the local police involved.

He stood on the patio, the dolphins once again gracing him with their morning travels. As he watched them jump, splashing gracefully into the sea, he felt Hanna's arms reach around his waist from behind. Her cheek felt warm against his shoulders, and he hoped he'd be able to keep her safe.

A knock at the door startled him, and he looked at her quizzically, his eyebrows raised.

She shrugged her shoulders. "Not my house. Not that I know the visitors I get either," she said, smiling.

He opened the door, his eyes widening. "Captain. Good morning," he said, opening the door wider.

"Good morning, Colin. Sorry to disturb you." He tipped his hat and nodded toward Hanna. "Good morning, Hanna."

"Morning, Captain," she said. "Would you like some coffee?"

The captain cleared his throat as he twisted his hat in his hands. "I'm afraid I'm on official business. Brought some company. Colin, the Delegado would like to talk with you. About the fires."

Colin knew the local Delagado, the South Campos appointee responsible for disagreements and anything criminal. He'd met Senor Jimenez several times at fire scenes.

"Oh, great, sir," Colin said, smiling at Hanna. "We've found some things that might be of interest."

The captain shifted from one foot to another, looking uncomfortable. With his eyes lowered, he said, "Son, I think you'd better just answer their questions today."

Colin's brows furrowed as he looked from the Captain to Hanna. Her face was expressionless as she moved to the computer, seemingly straightening the desk up and placing the prints of the photographs in stacks. She turned off the computer, quickly placed a book on top of the photographs, grabbed her coffee and sat on the couch.

The Delgado strode in the front door, a uniformed police officer behind him.

"Hello, Colin," he said, extending his hand with a wide smile.

Colin shook his hand, stealing a glance at the

captain who now sat on a barstool at the counter. "Hello, Senor Jimenez. What can I do for you?"

"We have been asking questions about the fires. Three fires in almost as many days is very many," he said, leaning against the kitchen counter. He folded his arms over his chest. "I hear that you have done a good job with the fires, and have been back afterward to investigate." He peered at Colin from under the brim of his hat, his eyes narrowed.

"Yes, sir, I have."

"Why did you return to the fire scenes? We are to investigate those, as you know."

"I'm sorry, sir. I was a bit confused about the cause, and the homeowners asked me to take a look. I didn't mean to compromise any investigation."

"Did you find anything of interest that I should know about?"

Colin hesitated a moment, glancing at Hanna. Her gaze was steady, her dark eyes meeting his, and he felt he knew what he should do.

"No, sir. I've found nothing so far," he said, squaring his shoulders. "I don't really even know what I'm looking for. I'm just a volunteer firefighter. An amateur."

Senor Jimenez rested his hands on the counter as

he leveled his gaze at Colin. After a few moments, he said, "How long have you lived here, Colin?"

"About five years, sir."

"And where did you move here from?" The Delgado pushed himself from the counter and began to walk back and forth, pacing.

"Ireland, sir."

"Yes, I've heard that. And I've heard other things that I've never felt need to speak of. Is it true that you have experience with fires in a way that might be...harmful?"

Colin's face fell into his hands as he shook his head. "No, no, no. I've never been involved in anything like that, sir. It's a rumor that I just can't shake," he said, his voice rising.

The captain stood, crossing the room and placing his hands on Colin's shoulders. "Relax, son, he's just asking questions."

Breathing deeply, Colin looked at the Delgado. "Sir, this is my home. I have no reason to do anyone harm. I've spent my time here trying to help. And that's what I plan to continue doing."

Senor Jimenez stopped pacing. He took his hat off, tossing it on the counter. "Colin, I'm in a bad spot here. I need you to be honest with me."

"Anything, sir," Colin said as he looked from the Delgado to the captain. "Anything I can do to help."

The captain cleared his throat, and the Delgado nodded at him.

"Colin, we've had homeowners report that they've seen a car at the fire scenes, both before and after. Before the fires started, and then later afterward."

Hanna sat up, leaning forward. She rested her chin in her hand, her eyes on Colin.

"Is that so, Captain? Is that someone we can find and ask questions of? That would be helpful."

The captain and Delegado looked at each other, and then back to Colin. "The car is yours, son. The only blue Jeep with flames painted on the side that we know of in the South Campos."

Colin sat down hard on the couch beside Hanna, his breath catching in his throat.

"Captain, Senor Jimenez, I can assure you that I had nothing to do with these fires. Nothing at all. In fact— "

"The fire yesterday was at my house," Hanna interrupted. "We were both injured. Why would he possibly have anything to do with that?" She stood, her hands on her hips, challenging the statements she'd just heard.

The Delgado slowly walked to the counter, picking up his hat and slowly turned to Colin. “I don’t know yet. All I know right now is that you are considered a suspect, and I must ask you not to leave the south campos until this matter is investigated.”

CHAPTER 23

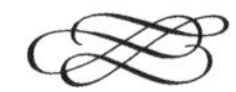

Silence enveloped Colin and Hanna as they watched the cars disappear in the distance. Nala whimpered at Colin's feet as Hanna pulled him inside the house, shutting the door fast behind her.

"We've got to do something. I don't know who saw that car besides us, but they reported it, and now we have to—"

"What? Do what?" Colin said, sitting on the couch with a thud. With his elbows on his knees, his head fell into his hands. "It's all coming back to haunt me, Hanna. I thought I was through with it all."

She paced quickly in front of the fireplace, its warm glow gone. "I couldn't help thinking while they were talking...kept remembering something. I can't quite pin it."

"What do you mean?" His shoulders still hunched, he couldn't understand what she was getting at.

"Last night, when you had me smell the can of lacquer, I remembered smelling it before. I just can't remember where."

Colin thought for a moment. "You smelled it when I was painting the mural. Your nose crinkled the same way," he said, a smile spreading against his will.

"Not then," she said. "Another time. Recently."

Colin stood slowly and rubbed the back of his neck. He snapped his fingers suddenly and smiled. "I remember it, too." Grabbing his coat from the back of the chair, he grasped her hand and pulled her toward the door. "Come on. We've got to go."

Nala jumped in the car before Hanna could get in the passenger seat, taking her usual position in the back.

"Where are we going?" She held onto the strap on the side of the window as he spun out of the drive-way. "What's the hurry?"

"Do you remember that shack we saw when we

were riding the other day? The one on the side of the creek bed?"

"Yes. The one with the smoke coming out of it?" She hit the dashboard with her hand. "You're right. That's where I noticed that smell."

"Do you remember the car that was outside of it?"

She thought for a moment. "Oh, my gosh. It was just like yours. Without the flames."

"Exactly," he said, turning the car onto the paved highway and heading south. "Do you think you can remember where it is, by car?"

She straightened the cap on her head and looked out to the west, to the mountains. "Sure. I've been by there many times. Slow down a little. The turn is right up here." She pointed to a large elephant tree a bit ahead. "Right here."

Colin slowed and turned the Jeep hard right as he headed into the soft sand of the creek bed. Following the twists and turns of the dry wash, he tried to imagine who could be doing this, who would want to frame him.

"Slow down, Speed Racer. You're going to miss it," she said, smiling.

"Okay, okay. I just want to see what's going on here."

"So do I, but I want to get there in one piece." Her knuckles white, she hadn't let go of the strap since they'd left the house. "There it is," she said, pointing up to the top of the arroyo.

Colin cut the engine, coasting to a stop under a mesquite tree out of view from the shack. No smoke was coming from the chimney and they walked slowly up the bank.

As they crested the bank, he held his finger to his mouth, holding Hanna back behind him. "I don't see a car or any movement," he said. "But I do smell lacquer thinner."

"So do I," she said, her nose crinkling once again.

He grabbed her hand as they walked slowly toward the shack. Its door hung off the top hinge and several of the slats had fallen off the sides. "Stay here. I'll see what I can see in the window," he said, crouching and moving forward slowly. He put his hands up to the lone window to the left of the door. "It's covered with something."

He motioned for her to join him, moving slowly to the door and lifting the rusty metal latch that held it closed. He tugged once more, the latch not budging an inch.

"Maybe it's locked from the inside," Hanna said,

peering around the corner to the side. "Is there another door?"

Tiptoeing around the back of the building, Colin held his hand up to Hanna behind him. He let out a whistle as he peered around the corner. "Would you look at this?"

Hanna peered around his shoulder. "Oh, my God," she said, her hand over her mouth.

The shed had been built into the dune behind it, and a large alcove had been dug into the hill to the side. Inside, rows of cans lined a makeshift shelf. Lacquer thinner, gasoline, propane, even lighter fluid for barbecues stood all in cans inside the alcove. To the right of the shelves stood an open metal barrel full of clean rags.

"What would somebody want with all this stuff way out here?" Hanna asked, her eyes scanning the shelves.

"I don't know, but I think it's not good." Colin turned back to the shed. "I've got to find a way in there."

"Let's check the other side for a door. Or break the window." Hanna made her hand into a fist and thumped it into her palm.

Colin smiled. "Let's not get carried away, shall we? I'm sure there's an easier method."

"Okay, but I'm ready," Hanna said, pulling her baseball cap further down her forehead.

They moved around to the west side of the shack, another door with a metal latch in its center. Hanna crept up behind Colin as he jiggled the latch. "They can't be rusted shut. It's only been a few days since we saw a car here."

Hanna picked up a rock and, in one swift move, hit the latch from underneath. She jumped back as it flew open. "See? It was just stuck. I told you, we're going in there."

"Easy there, lass," Colin said. "I'm going in first."

Colin squinted as he entered the building, his eyes adjusting to the darkness. He felt on the wall for a light switch and, finding none, took his flashlight out of his pocket.

"God, it smells awful in here," Hanna said as she pinched her nose.

"Yeah, not good at all." Colin shone the flashlight around the room slowly, catching his breath as his heart began to race. Several milk crates lined the counter to the left and he moved closer, reaching his hand inside.

"Timers?" Hanna asked, as she turned her flashlight in the direction of the crates.

Colin placed the devices back into the box. "Yeah,

I'm afraid so." As he turned to move further into the shed, Hanna's flashlight clattered onto the floor.

"What? What is it?" He spun around and stared at Hanna. She stood stock still, staring down at the wall in front of her. He followed her gaze, and his heart skipped a beat.

The bulletin board had several pictures on it. With the low light from the door, he was able to make out photographs. Slowly, he realized that there were four pictures, all familiar.

"That's the house where the first fire was," Hanna said as she pointed to the first picture on the left. "And that's Mike's house in Playa Luna."

"The second fire," James said slowly. His eyes widened as Hanna gasped.

"There's a picture of my house," she said, her eyes brimming with tears.

His stomach clenched as he turned to the fourth picture on the bulletin board.

"Oh, goodness," he said.

Hanna stared, not blinking. "Isn't that the resort?"

"It is, I'm afraid."

He reached up and stopped her as she started to take the pictures off of the board. "No, we don't want anyone to know we were here, Hanna."

She looked at him and nodded. As she backed away from the pictures, her foot caught on something on the floor. She fell into Colin, her flashlight clattering on the floor.

Colin steadied her, bending to pick up her flashlight. As he stood, his light caught something under the table, its bright colors catching his eye. "What is that?" he said, handing her the flashlight.

Slowly, she reached under the table and picked up two big magnetic decals for the side of a car. They matched the flames that he and James had painted on his blue Jeep during their drunken fiesta. Matched them exactly.

"So, what are we going to do now?" Hanna said after she'd finally caught her breath. She'd dropped the decals as if they'd burned her and run out the door, Colin close behind, and not stopped until she'd gotten to the car.

"I have no idea." Colin's head spun as he raced toward the highway through the creek bed, and he let out a laugh.

"Why are you laughing? This is anything but funny." She couldn't believe he was laughing. Framed for arson? And laughing?

"I know it's not funny, Hanna. I just never, ever thought I'd be in this sort of trouble. Again."

CHAPTER 24

James and Alex were both at Colin's house as he and Hanna pulled up. "They got here quickly," Hanna said.

"We don't lay about when we get an emergency call on the radio," Colin said, smiling.

Colin poured tequila as they all settled in for the story. "Not too much now, James. We've got a mystery to solve," he said as he handed James his shot glass.

"I'm not that bad, mate. I'm ready," he said as he lifted his glass. "Now, tell us what this is all about."

Colin quickly recounted what the pictures had revealed and showed them the wires and timers. He explained about the pictures he'd taken at the previous fire sites, and that he and Hanna thought that the arsonist came back to take out the incendiary devices before anybody noticed.

"It's the disadvantage of being a volunteer brigade. We can only get to things when we have a chance, and if we suspect something," Colin said as he finished describing what they'd found.

"Bloody hell, who would do such a thing?" James asked, his eyes wide and fists clenching.

"I have no idea, mate, but there's more." Colin described the visit from the captain and the Delegado, complete with the request that he not leave the South Campos.

Alex laughed loudly. "You can't be serious, amigo. They suspect you?"

Hanna set chips and salsa on the table, taking a seat next to Colin. "He mentioned Colin's questionable past," she said, taking a sip of tequila. "He didn't seem to be joking."

"Well, the biggest red flag is that there has been a blue Jeep spotted at the arson sites that looks a lot like mine."

Hanna cut in. "Not a lot like. Exactly like, with the same paint color and the flames on the side. But it can't be Colin's Jeep. It just can't be. We found magnets, like those big ones for realtors or whatever, that made it look just like Colin's. Not a real paint job."

After hearing the rest of the story, complete with the magnets just like the flames on Colin's car, James pounded his empty glass on the table. "That's it. I'm not going to take this. Nobody's going to copy my flame paintings."

"Oh, brother," Colin said, rolling his eyes at his friend. "All kidding aside, it gets more serious. We found four pictures in the shack. Three of the structures have already been burned. There is one more."

Hanna and Colin turned to Alex, who was listening intently. "What? The resort?" he asked, his eyebrows raised in shock.

"Yes, that's what we believe. It's the only one of the four places that hasn't yet been attacked."

Alex rubbed his chin as he looked from James to Colin. "What exactly was the picture of? Any specific part of the resort?"

"Yes, the stable," Hanna said. "We believe that's where this person will strike next."

Colin pushed back from the table, his arms folded over his chest. "I know that it's the resort at risk, Alex, but with your permission and James' help, I'd like to try to catch this guy. And clear my name."

"I'll do whatever you need to help stop this threat, once and for all. Cassie and I have put our hearts and souls into this, and too much damage has been done already," Alex said, his kind eyes turning to Hanna. "I'm just grateful no one has been hurt so far."

James filled their glasses with tequila once more. Raising his glass, he said, "Count me in. Here's to catching the guy."

CHAPTER 25

The stables at the resort were quiet, tranquil, when Colin and James arrived the next day.

"Doesn't look like anything's been planted here." Colin wiped his hands on his pants, removing the dirt from crawling all over the stables, rafters included. Nala ran around in circles. "I know, girl, but you wouldn't have liked it up there." Colin reached down and gave her a quick pat before Nala ran off to find a stick for Colin to throw.

James wiped his forehead with a handkerchief as he looked around the inside of the stables. "Nothing outside either, mate. Maybe he's not been here yet."

"These fires have all happened within days of each other. I have no doubt that whatever is going to happen here will happen soon. I was just positive that we'd find something already." Colin rubbed the back of his neck and stared through the open stable window toward the construction of the main resort. "All of the other fires were set by explosives, set off remotely. I just think maybe we're missing something."

"I checked inside every stall and in the tack room. I didn't see any propane tanks."

"Don't forget it's not just propane tanks we're looking for. Any big cans of any kind?"

Colin headed toward the big doors of the tack room. "Let's look in here one more time. I'm not willing to give up on this."

Moving through the tack room slowly, James started on one side and Colin on the other. They lifted the saddles, opened every drawer and checked in every cupboard. Against the back wall, water tanks stood in a row, waiting to be filled when the horses arrived the following week. A small door led from the tack room to the feed room that had been empty when Hanna and Colin had visited days before.

"Did you check in there?" James asked, gesturing to the room that would hold the hay and alfalfa. "I didn't."

Shaking his head slowly, Colin moved toward the door, reaching out to lift the latch. He stopped suddenly, pulling his hand back quickly.

"What is it?" James moved toward Colin but stopped as Colin held up his hand, raising a finger to his mouth, motioning for James to be silent. He pointed to Nala, who had been sitting at the door at alert, staring at the crack.

"Nala, come," Colin said, motioning for the dog to move away from the door. She looked up at him with a whimper, immediately turning her head back to the door, refusing to move.

Colin cleared his throat. "I was in there the other day," Colin said. His jaw tightened as James looked at him, a question in his eyes. "I know the horses aren't coming for another week. Nothing in there. Let's go take another look outside," he said, motioning for James to follow him to the door.

As they left the room, Colin turned toward Nala once again. "Nala, we're leaving. Come," he said, continuing to the far end of the stable and the exit. "Just follow me, James. "

The long, rectangular stables had entrances at each end and they moved quickly toward the door furthest away from the tack room. As they reached the far end, they stopped, turning back to Nala's frantic barking. Through the corridor of the stable, Nala's barks echoed and they watched as a man tried to rush out the opposite door as Nala nipped at his heels.

"Knock it off, you stupid dog," the man said as he tried to kick Nala away from him. He wore a black baseball cap and a black handkerchief was tied around his nose and mouth, obscuring his face.

Colin and James ran toward the man as he turned and tried to run out the opposite door. He couldn't have seen the flames shoot from the tack room, nor heard the explosion that followed before he was knocked to the ground by the falling beams of the roof of the stable.

CHAPTER 26

The unconscious man and Nala had both been knocked by the blast to the far side of the stable as flames began to take over the tack room. Colin winced as he heard Nala whine.

"Call in to the bomberos, James." Colin moved as close to the fire as he could. His forearm covering his face, he moved toward where the man was lying pinned beneath two large beams, still unconscious. "Nala," he shouted, not able to see her amid the rubble. Grabbing one of the beams with both hands, he dug his heels in the ground and tried to lift the beam off of the man, flames inching closer.

"They're on their way, Colin," James said, rushing to grab the beam. On the count of three, they both pulled up on the sturdy wood. It didn't budge.

"We're not going to get that off of him, mate," Colin said, looking around for something to use as a lever.

"I think I can help," Hanna said as she walked in, Violet's lead in her hand as the large mare walked in behind her.

"What are you doing here? It's not safe," Colin shouted as the fire grew bigger, its flames roaring. "It's not safe, Hanna. Horses panic at fires," he said, his hands held up in front of him blocking her from coming further.

"Not this horse, Colin. I told you before. I have rope, and Violet can pull off the beams," she said as she threw one end of the rope toward Collin and tied the other to Violet's saddle.

James and Colin wrapped the rope around the beams several times, securing it with a tight knot. Colin turned to Hanna, nodding. She patted Violet as she moved to take her lead, speaking softly to her as she pulled her forward.

Violet strained to pull the beam, her eyes trained on Hanna. Colin and James each grabbed the beam to try to move it, the flames now reaching the far end of the beam.

"Hurry, Hanna, we're running out of time," James shouted as he and Colin pulled on the beam.

Hanna didn't pull harder on Violet's lead, but turned to look at her. Her eyes met the mare's. She spoke softly once more, and turned to walk away from the beam. Violet let out a loud whinny, rose up on her hind legs and leapt forward, pulling the beam off of and away from the man as James helped push it further.

Hanna quickly untied the rope from the saddle and led Violet back toward the man. James and Colin had pulled him from the fire and lifted him, placing him over the saddle.

"James, take him outside with Hanna," Colin said, his eyes darting about the fire for Nala. He finally spotted her and quickly lifted her away from the fire, running after James and Hanna just as another explosion rocked the stable.

CHAPTER 27

A wet tongue on his face was the first thing Colin felt as he slowly came to consciousness. A groan escaped his lips as he wiggled his toes and fingers, wondering why he felt like he'd been hit by a truck. As his eyelids fluttered open, he heard Hanna gasp. "James, he's awake."

Nala continued licking his cheek until he was able to give her a quick, reassuring pat. "Nala, that's enough. I'm fine."

"What happened? I don't remember anything after finding Nala and running." He ran his hand over his face, gingerly fingering a swollen eyelid.

Hanna held his hand, her eyes brimming with tears. She wiped them away with her shirt sleeve as she pulled Nala away, holding her in her arms and sitting with a thud on the ground next to Colin. "I'm so relieved, Colin. We weren't sure how you were, and the ambulances haven't arrived yet."

"Good one, mate, saving Nala," James said, bending down to pat her head. Nala wriggled in Hanna's arms, trying to break free and get to Colin.

"Please, don't move until they get here." Hanna's voice was almost a whisper.

Colin squeezed her hand as he brushed away the remaining tears. "You saved that man's life, Hanna. You and Violet."

"I'm so glad I could help," she said, glancing at Violet tied up to a nearby tree, away from the fire.

"And she saved yours too, mate," James added, his arm around Hanna. "She took Violet back in and we had to take you out the same way we did the bad guy."

Colin sat up slowly, holding his hand up as Hanna began to protest. Their eyes met briefly as he smiled, continuing to assess the damage he knew he'd sustained. "I'm okay. Really. The fire is out?"

James stood, hands on his hips as he watched the bomberos finish the fire off. "The boys were here in time to save half of the stable, but the paramedics are still on their way from town. Our bad guy is still unconscious. We've just left him be for the moment."

"Who is he?" Colin slowly stood up and headed in the direction of the man who had burnt so many buildings, risked lives and tried to ruin his own.

"Don't know yet. Still wearing that mask," James said. "I made sure he was breathing all right and tended to you."

The man started to stir as the three slowly approached him, his groans audible over the approaching sirens of the ambulances. Colin reached out, gently removing the black bandana covering his face, revealing Bruce, the older fisherman who'd been around the south campos for decades.

"Well, I'll be darned," Alex said as he approached the group from behind. "I knew they didn't like the resort, but had no idea they'd go to this length to stop it."

Hanna looped her arm through Colin's as he clenched his fists, his jaw tightening. "Colin, not all people understand the bigger picture. Leave him be, for now."

The paramedics arrived quickly, ushering the four away as they tended to the man, treating his burns and administering oxygen.

"I just don't understand. I've heard talk from these old boys for years about the good old days, how the fish used to jump in your boat and there were no phones, televisions or radios. But to blame the resort for all the changes?" Colin said, his head shaking slowly as he watched the paramedics. "And to blame me?"

Alex gave Colin a pat on the back. "Bruce and his friends found this part of Baja at a different time, my friend. It was a different type of paradise for them then, a true getaway from civilization entirely. In my business, it is a constant challenge to convince residents that what we are doing will make things better in the long run."

Bruce had been loaded onto a gurney and the paramedics wheeled him toward the ambulance. The federal police had arrived and were walking along side as the paramedics prepared to load him in the ambulance.

Colin walked toward the ambulance slowly, holding Hanna's hand and pulling her along. "What are you going to do, Colin? There's nothing you can do that will help."

Colin stood beside the injured man, determined to understand why he'd done this. "Bruce, why would you do this? Why did you do this?"

Bruce groaned, rubbing a sooty hand over his forehead. "You boys know that. Too many people, too much commotion. I wanted it to be the way it used to be. Fish enough for all, quiet enough for thinking."

He turned his face away as Colin pressed on. "You know as well as I do that fish have been dwindling here for years. Sport fishermen and commercial alike have changed the whole Sea of Cortez. But the resort is an ecological preserve, trying to change all that for the future of all of us."

"So they say," Bruce grumbled. "Don't want it, don't need it. Wanted them out."

Hanna shook her head slowly. "You had to know you couldn't get away with this, Bruce. And you're lucky nobody was badly hurt. Is that what you wanted?"

Bruce turned to her, his eyes moist. "Young lady, I never intended to hurt anyone. Just wanted them to go away." He wiped his sleeve across his face, turning away again. Colin, I never meant to hurt you, either. It just kind of got away from me, that's all. Figured with your history and all, you'd be a better suspect than me."

"My history?" Colin folded his arms across his chest.

"Well, you know. IRA bomber and all," Bruce said. "Thought they'd look at you first and leave me alone. Never thought you boys would catch on, and I did my best not to hurt anyone."

Alex groaned and James snickered as Bruce was loaded into the ambulance, the police quickly taking notes of the conversation.

Colin spun on his heel. "You all think this is funny, do ya?"

James held his hands up as Hanna tried to hide a smile. "No, of course not. But, seriously, that urban myth has followed you quite awhile. Maybe now, it can be put to rest.

"Maybe so. And the damage has been property only. Buildings are buildings and can be re-built. No one was badly hurt, and you boys stopped the craziness. Well done," Alex said, extending his hand to Colin.

Shaking Alex's hand, Colin's eyes met Hanna's. Her face softened, and she pulled him forward for a hug. "Nicely done, Colin. Thank you for ending this," she whispered in his ear.

"And thanks for saving my life, Hanna." Alex and James turned away as their embrace turned into a gentle kiss.

CHAPTER 28

Colorful Mexican blankets billowed on tables set in front of the newly-built stable at the Rancho Del Sol resort. People from all over the South Campos sat under shade covers, enjoying homemade tortillas, salsas, beans and rice for the second attempt at the fundraiser for the bomberos. A breeze cooled the air as it swept off the waves and the sun shimmered over the water. A roar came up from the crowd as the band started into the Rolling Stones tune that had been interrupted by the explosions several months ago.

James and Megan set down a round of tequila as Hanna and Colin finished one of many dances during the festival. Hanna's black hair swung in the breeze, her colorful skirt twirling over her red cowboy boots, her head thrown back in laughter.

"They're quite a pair, aren't they?" Megan said, reaching for James's hand.

"Well, they sure know how to live it up." James laughed, tapping his foot in time to the music. "Want to dance?"

"No, thanks, I like my feet un-smashed." Megan laughed at his wounded expression, smoothing his bearded cheek with her hand. "There are many things I love about you, James, but dancing isn't one of them."

"I'll get better if I practice," he said as Colin and Hanna returned to the table.

Hanna plopped down on her seat, a breath escaping as she did. "It's a lot of work, James. Highly overrated," she said, nudging Colin with her elbow. "Especially if you're learning Irish dancing."

"Hey, now, you love it," Colin said, his eyes twinkling.

They applauded as the band ended the song, Colin's eyes trained on Alex as he took the microphone offered by the lead guitarist.

"Thank you for coming, everyone," he said, his wide smile gleaming across the audience. "I have rarely known a community that offers so much support to one another, and I am proud to be a part of it all."

James nudged Megan and winked, her eyes growing wide. Her mouth silently shaped the word, "What?" He shrugged his shoulders and pointed again to Alex.

"It is with a full heart that I would like to express my gratitude to the volunteer bomberos, the captain and his men who tirelessly work to keep our community safe. I would especially like to thank James, Colin and Hanna who have gone above and beyond to eliminate a threat from our community, and who saved many structures from further damage and risked their lives in the process. "

The crowd rose in a standing ovation, nodding their heads toward the table where Hanna, Colin and James all blushed.

As the applause died down, Alex continued. "Captain, would you join me, please?"

The Captain's confused expression was hidden by a smile, as he glanced around at the crowd and walked toward the stage. As he reached the microphone, Alex looked to the back of the crowd, giving a nod to his assistants in the back of the field.

Turning to the captain, he said, "Captain, it is my honor to present these gifts to you and the bomberos, on behalf of myself, Cassie and the Rancho Del Sol resort, as only a small token of our gratitude to you for your bravery and commitment to the safety of the South Campos."

Hanna jumped as she heard the sound of sirens from behind the stable. Colin's mouth hung open as two new, state-of-the-art fire engines drove out from behind the stables, slowly around the crowd and parked on each side of the stage.

Cassie dropped Alex's hand, clapping loudly, her smile beaming across the crowd. She winked as her eyes met Hanna's.

"I don't quite know what to say, Alex. 'Thanks' doesn't quite cut it," the captain answered, the keys to both trucks now in his hands. "Let's check them out, boys." He shook Alex's hand warmly as the crowd cheered once again.

Colin sat, stunned, as Alex and Cassie made their way over to their table. Alex raised his hand, signaling for a server to bring another round of drinks.

"That's mighty generous of you, Alex," James said as he shook Alex's hand vigorously. "We sure needed that, eh, Colin? No more spit and duct tape on the old ones."

"It's the least we could do, gentlemen. The bomberos are what keep us safe down here."

Cassie smiled warmly at Hanna and Colin as the server set down glasses for all. "I have another announcement, if it's okay," she said, raising her glass. "I'd like to make a toast to our new stable manager and resort riding instructor, Hanna." She nodded to Hanna and Colin as she squeezed Alex's hand.

Hanna blushed as Colin turned to her, his eyes wide. "You couldn't find anybody better. She's the horse whisperer," he said, his eyes not leaving hers.

"Salut!" Megan said, as they all raised their glasses to the future.

EPILOGUE

The warm water of the Sea of Cortez lapped at his feet as he sat in the sand and studied the horizon. It had been a wonderful day, and Colin was enjoying the warm feeling of belonging that had taken residence inside him lately.

"Penny for your thoughts," Hanna said as she walked up behind him. She took off her shoes and threw them behind her, lifting her skirt a bit and wiggling her toes in the gentle waves.

"While I normally don't think much of anything, certainly nothing worth more than a penny, I was just thinking how lucky I was to have met you. And that I might never have done without these fires. Without all of the bad things that happened, none of the good things would have, either." He turned back to the horizon for a moment and then shook his head. "I'm really happy for you and your new position with the resort. You're perfect for the job."

"It would be a dream come true to work with the horses, to raise and train them the way I believe it should be done. And to educate others who come to the resort about how horses can really be." Her hand played with the hem of her shirt and she turned to face him. "The only drawback is that I would have to live on the resort and we would no longer be neighbors."

He grabbed her hand and pulled her down to sit next to him. "Hanna, I have something to tell you myself. I've been waiting, but now seems a good time.

Her brows furrowed as her eyes met his.

"Alex and Cassie had a proposition for me, as well." He took a deep breath and continued. "He's asked me to be fire marshal for the resort. No more painting. I would be a professional firefighter."

Hanna clapped her hands, a smile spreading wide across her face. She jumped to her feet, pulling him up with her.

"Colin, that's wonderful. Congratulations," she said. "I am thrilled."

She looked genuinely pleased at the news, and his

heart soared. Now, if only he could tell her the rest of it. He'd mulled it over for days, but the more he thought about it, the more certain he'd become. And as he watched her laugh, her spirit light, he knew he was right.

"Hanna, there's something else."

She turned toward him and took his hand, her smile fading a bit. He didn't mean to alarm her, and hoped what he had to say would put her smile back where it belonged. He'd just have to get over the fear that someone so special might not feel the same way he did.

He closed his eyes and felt her warm palm on his face. He took a deep breath and figured it was now or never.

"He's offered me a casita to live in," he began slowly, kicking himself that he couldn't get this all out faster. He'd never had much trouble talking—sometimes too much—but for some reason he was tongue-tied at the moment.

"Fantastic," she said. "We could be neighbors. Maybe we could ask him if our casitas could be next to each other. That would be fun, wouldn't it? I could feed Nala sometimes and we could spend lots of time together."

He took another deep breath and rested his

finger on her lips. At least one of them wasn't tongue-tied, but he needed to forge ahead regardless.

Her eyes widened and she stopped talking, looking up at him quizzically.

"I don't want to be your neighbor, Hanna. We've been through so much together, and I couldn't have done any of this without you. And I don't want to do anything without you anymore. Hanna, I love you. And no, I don't want you to be my neighbor. I want you to be more than that. I want you to be my wife."

Hanna dropped his hand and took a step back. His heart stopped beating for more than a moment, and didn't start again until a slow smile spread across her face, and she moved forward, throwing her arms around his neck.

She nestled her cheek against his neck, and when she pulled back, his shirt was wet and she swiped at her eyes.

"Colin, there's nothing in this world that would make me happier. I love you, too. You have shown me that the world is kind, and safe and I want to be part of yours. It wouldn't be the same without you in it."

He reached for her, but she turned toward the sea, her arms lifted up and her eyes closed. She didn't speak, but he could hear her in his heart thanking the sun, the sky and even the spirits, and he knew that they were meant to be together.

She turned back toward him, her arms around his neck again as she stood on her tiptoes and lifted her chin up, kissing him soundly. He pulled her tight, comforted that he would never have to let her go.

Hanna's hair blew in the breeze as she threw her head back and laughed, her colorful skirt dancing about her knees. She twirled, stopping in front of him.

"You look like a regular Irish dancer," Colin said. Her beauty still amazed him, and now he knew she was as beautiful inside as out. He pulled her toward him, feeling warmth spread as she rested her head on his shoulder.

Her breathing slowed as she looked up and into his eyes. "Do you remember when we rode the horses out to the fossil mounds? I told you then that the spirits move strangely here."

"Yes, I do. But I had no idea how wonderful that would be, how much my life would change."

Hanna smiled as she grabbed his hand, pulling him back toward the fiesta. "Let's go see what's waiting for us next."

He laughed as he ran behind her, wondering what would be next. He realized he couldn't wait to find out.

THE END

I HOPE YOU ENJOYED AS BY THE LIGHT OF THE MOON!

Next in this series:

As Blue As The Sky

I'd also like to introduce you to the first book in my new women's fiction series:

Newport Harbor House

If you'd like to receive an email about my new releases,
please join my mailing list.

ABOUT THE AUTHOR

Cindy Nichols writes heartwarming stories interwoven with the bonds of friendship and family that combine what she loves most about women's fiction and romance.

Cindy lives in and loves everything about the southwest, from its deserts and mountains to the sea. She discovered her passion for writing after a twenty-year career in education. When she's not writing, she travels as much as she can with her children who, although adults, still need her no matter what they think.

Feel free to sign up for her list to hear about new releases as soon as they are available as well as extras like early bird discounts. Click here to sign up: Cindy's Email List

Made in the USA
San Bernardino, CA
29 July 2020